SCREAM SHOP

War of the Trolls

By Tr...

CH

To my sister Anna. With her charisma
and ability, she can achieve anything
she puts her mind to.
—B.D.

Copyright © 2004 by Tracey West. Illustrations copyright © 2004 by Brian W. Dow. All rights reserved. Published by Grosset & Dunlap, a division of Penguin Young Readers Group, 345 Hudson Street, New York, New York 10014. GROSSET & DUNLAP is a trademark of Penguin Group (USA) Inc. Printed in the U.S.A.

Library of Congress Cataloging-in-Publication Data

West, Tracey, 1965–
  War of the trolls / by Tracey West ; illustrated by Brian W. Dow.
    p. cm. — (Scream shop ; 8)
  Summary: When Sean, a devoted bookworm, buys a strange-looking fantasy novel from Sebastian Cream's Junk Shop, he ignores the book's warning and reads it after midnight, when he is drawn into a world of terrifying trolls.
  ISBN 0-448-43557-8 (pbk.)
  1. Plot-your-own stories. [1. Trolls—Fiction. 2. Books and reading—Fiction. 3. Horror stories. 4. Plot-your-own stories.] I. Dow, Brian, ill. II. Title.
  PZ7.W51727War 2004
  [Fic]—dc22

                              2004014028

ISBN 0-448-43557-8   10 9 8 7 6 5 4 3 2 1

S.CREAM SHOP

War of the Trolls

By Tracey West

Illustrated by Brian W. Dow

Grosset & Dunlap • New York

"What's up, Worm?"

Sean Flatbush's older brother, Jake, gave him a playful punch in the arm as he walked into the kitchen. Sean didn't answer. He slowly spooned cereal into his mouth and kept reading his book, the last in the *Lord of the Rings* trilogy.

"Jake, I don't want you to call your brother that," Mrs. Flatbush scolded. She sat at the kitchen table next to Sean, cutting up a banana for the youngest Flatbush, three-year-old Henry.

Jake grabbed a carton of milk from the refrigerator. "What else am I supposed to call him? He's got his face in a book every time I see him. Won't even say good morning. He's a total bookworm."

"Worm!" Henry repeated, happily squishing banana slices in his fist.

Mrs. Flatbush sighed. "Your brother has a point, Sean. Why don't you put down that book while you're eating?"

"But I'm almost done!" Sean whined. "Besides, reading is good for you."

"Of course it is," Mrs. Flatbush said, gently pushing the book down on the table. "But you need to spend time doing other things, too."

Sean knew better than to argue with his mother. He closed the book and began shoveling cereal into his mouth as quickly as he could.

"May I be excused now?" Sean asked.

"Of course," Mrs. Flatbush said. "What are you doing today?"

"I'm going to finish my book and then go down to the library," Sean replied.

"Aren't you going to the school carnival?" Jake asked. "I'm going with J.T. You can come with us if you want."

Sean gave his mom a pleading look. "Do I have to?"

Mrs. Flatbush shook her head. "I don't think there's a child on this Earth who would rather go to the library than a carnival. But if that's what makes you happy . . ."

"Thanks!" Sean said quickly. He jumped up from the table, grabbing his book. "I'll be home soon."

Sean only had a few paragraphs left to go, so he decided to read them while he walked to the library, to save time. His mother hated when he did that. Sean was careful to stop at each street corner, but he did bump into a few trees on the way. He always did.

Ms. Dietz, the librarian, smiled when Sean entered. "Don't tell me you've finished so soon?"

she asked.

Sean nodded and placed the book on the librarian's desk. "What else have you got for me?"

Ms. Dietz frowned. "I was worried this might happen, Sean," she said. "You see, you've read every fantasy book in the children's section and now the YA section. We're not getting any new shipments until next week."

Sean struggled to accept the news. No more books? How was he supposed to get through the weekend?

"Are you sure?" Sean asked.

"I'm sorry," the librarian said. "Maybe you'd like to try another genre. Like mystery. Or science fiction."

"No, thanks," Sean mumbled. He didn't like books that took place in the present, or in the future with shiny robots and lasers. He liked the magical settings of fantasy books and the way they made him feel like he was part of the adventure.

"I'm sure I can recommend something . . ." Ms. Dietz was saying, but Sean wasn't listening. He was already digging through his pockets, trying to come up with another plan.

He had some cash leftover from his birthday money. Maybe his mom or dad would take him to that big bookstore on the highway. He'd be sure to find something new there.

Sean said good-bye to Ms. Dietz and left the library. As he walked home, he plotted the best way to convince his parents to take him to the store.

Then something caught his eye. He stopped.

He was standing in front of a store called Sebastian Cream's Junk Shop. Sean had never seen it before. There were strange things displayed in the window: a stuffed badger angrily bearing its teeth, a dressmaker's dummy, a wooden chest carved with mysterious inscriptions, and stacks and stacks of old books.

Sean didn't hesitate. He quickly entered the store. There had to be some fantasy books here.

"May I help you?" asked the shop owner. The man was about as tall as Sean, with a ring of white hair around his head. If Sean hadn't been in such a hurry, he might have noticed that the man had unusually green eyes behind his glasses.

"Books," Sean said simply. The man nodded and pointed to a corner of the shop, filled with cardboard boxes.

"I'm sure you'll find something you'll like," he said.

Sean hurried to the boxes and began riffling through them. There were books on birds of the world, books filled with maps of forgotten countries, books filled with pictures of arcane-looking symbols.

Then Sean saw it. A leather-bound book with the title stamped in red: *War of the Trolls*.

Sean picked up the book. It was nice and thick—definitely a weekend's worth of reading. He read the title page. There was no author listed, but above the title were these words:

Warning. *Do not read this book after midnight.*

Sean was intrigued. It sounded like the beginning of a fantasy book to him. He flipped to the first page.

As the sun rose on the land of Liasa, the wizard stirred a potion over a blazing fire.

Sean kept reading, hooked, when he heard a little cough. He turned his head to see the shop-keeper standing behind him.

"Would you like to purchase the book?" he asked.

"Oh, sure," Sean said. "How much?"

The little man named a price, and Sean had enough in his pocket to cover it. As he left the shop, the store owner called out, "Read carefully!"

What a weird thing to say, Sean thought. But he quickly forgot about it and opened the book. He read all the way home, bumping into three more trees on the way. He read for the rest of the day, only stopping to eat lunch and dinner.

The first section of the book was about the

origin of a mystical land, Liasa. It was populated by magic-users and humans, until a mysterious ailment wiped out most of the magic in the land.

Sean wanted to keep reading after dinner, but his parents made him watch a movie with the rest of the family. After he went to bed, he kept reading under the covers with a flashlight so he wouldn't keep Henry awake.

Through his thin blanket, Sean could make out the time on his digital clock: 11:58. He paused, suddenly remembering the warning on the title page.

Do not read this book after midnight.

Just a gimmick, Sean told himself. He wasn't about to stop now. An army of trolls was amassing to attack Liasa. Things were just getting good.

Sean kept reading.

Suddenly, the words on the page began to swirl in front of his eyes. Sean blinked. He must have been getting tired.

But the words kept swirling. When they stopped again, Sean saw that they had formed a strange phrase on the page.

Bakari Liasa, revente azilla.

Sean blinked again. Was he seeing things? He must have turned the page without realizing it. Still, the words did not make any sense.

"Bakari Liasa, revente azilla?" Sean whispered

the words out loud.

That was when everything changed.

Sean was no longer in his bed, reading under the covers. He was standing underneath a gnarled tree next to a riverbank. A warm yellow sun shone above him.

And running toward him at full speed was a snarling, two-headed beast.

"I must be dreaming," Sean said.

But the beast kept coming.

A primitive survival instinct kicked in somewhere deep inside Sean. He had no idea what had happened. He just knew he had to get to safety—fast.

Sean looked up at the tree. He could climb—but what if the beast could climb, too?

Then there was the river. Sean could jump in. But what if the beast could swim?

If Sean jumps into the river, go to page 12.

If Sean climbs the tree, go to page 17.

Continued from page 11

Sean plunged into the river. The cold water chilled him, and he gasped, shuddering.

The two-headed beast stood on the shore, snarling and growling. It looked something like a dog, but its body was covered with shimmering green scales. Each of its two heads had a large snout filled with sharp teeth and two gleaming yellow eyes.

The beast was terrifying, but it didn't seem to be able to swim. Sean paddled on top of the water, trying to decide what to do.

He definitely wasn't dreaming. The cold water on his skin, the sun shining overhead—they were all too real.

So what had happened?

The warning on the book reverberated in Sean's mind.

Do not read this book after midnight.

Sean had read the book after midnight, and then those strange words had appeared, and Sean had read them aloud. Was that what had made this happen?

While Sean was thinking, he didn't notice that the current of the river had quickened pace, carrying him downstream. He tried to fight against it, straining to reach the shore on the other side. But he was too late.

The river carried him down a small, steep dip—and then he hit rapids. He managed to keep his head above water, but other than that, he had no control. The swirling water carried him farther and farther until the two-headed beast looked like a dot in the distance.

Through his panic, Sean tried to make sense of his surroundings. When he had first jumped into the river, the land around him had been covered by trees, but they seemed to be growing sparser the farther downstream he traveled. The landscape didn't look like anywhere he had ever been before. It certainly wasn't Bleaktown.

Finally, the current slowed down, and the river grew more shallow. Sean found he was able to swim again, to control where he was going.

But where was that?

"Hello?" Sean called out.

The riverbanks looked deserted. A few scraggly trees grew here and there, but they bore no leaves. No grass grew on the ground, which was covered with a reddish-brown dust. There didn't seem to be any sign of life.

Then Sean noticed, on one side of the river, what looked like a stone pathway. A pathway had to lead somewhere. Sean swam to the shore and climbed up onto the bank.

His cotton pajamas clung to his skin. The

dusty ground turned to mud under his bare feet and squished between his toes. Luckily, the sun was warm, and Sean knew he would dry out soon.

He headed out onto the stone path. The eerie quiet made him feel uneasy. *There has to be a reasonable explanation for what happened,* he thought. *Maybe I sleepwalked here.*

It wasn't a very convincing explanation, but Sean had nothing else to go on. In order to find out more, he'd have to find someone—anyone—to talk to.

Then, in the distance, he heard a voice.

"Help! Help!"

Sean picked up speed. The cry sounded like a boy his own age.

The path turned sharply, and Sean found himself on top of the hill.

He gasped.

A tall tree grew on top of the hill. A large, crudely built wooden cage hung from one of the branches. Inside the cage was a boy with sandy blond hair and a vest and pants that seemed to be made of animal skins. He looked shocked to see Sean.

"Get me out of here!" the boy cried. "They'll be back any minute!"

"What can I do?" Sean asked.

"The lock is on top of the cage," the boy answered. "Can you climb?"

Sean nodded. He had learned to climb the tall chestnut tree in his backyard years ago, when he wanted to find a quiet place for reading. He wasn't good at many sports, but he was a decent climber.

Sean shimmied up the tree. He crawled out onto the branch from which the cage dangled. There, on top of the cage, was a flat piece of wood slid into a bracket of some kind. Sean reached out and slid the wood back. Then he opened the lid of the cage.

The boy inside didn't hesitate. He scrambled up through the top of the cage.

"We've got to hurry," he said.

Sean didn't question him. He started back down the tree. The boy followed him. When the boy's feet touched the ground, he looked back and forth.

"Follow me," he said.

The boy started to run down the hill. Sean ran behind him. He had so many questions he wanted to ask, but the boy seemed to think getting out of the area was urgent.

Then Sean realized why.

A huge creature was stomping toward them up the hill. He looked sort of human, but he was as tall as the tree on the hill, and his skin was a sickly green. Huge muscles bulged on his arms and legs. Large, crooked teeth stuck out of his drooling mouth. He wore spiked leather bracelets on each wrist and a fur garment that draped over his shoulders and reached down below his waist. When he saw the boys, he let out a hideous cry.

The boy stopped abruptly, and a look of pure fear swept across his face.

"What should we do?" Sean asked.

If the boys run down the hill and past the troll, go to page 42.

If the boys run back up the hill, go to page 64.

Continued from page 11

Sean decided to climb the tree. He was an okay swimmer but a much better climber, thanks to the tall tree in his backyard. He often climbed up there to read so he could escape being bothered by his brothers. Sean scrambled up the tree as quickly as he could and anchored himself on a sturdy branch about twenty feet off the ground.

The beast charged the tree and stood on its hind legs. It looked something like a dog, but its body was covered with shimmering green scales. Each of its two heads had a large snout filled with sharp teeth and two gleaming yellow eyes. Sean watched in horror as the creature dug its claws into the bark of the tree and began to pull itself up the trunk.

"Help!" Sean cried. He looked frantically for another branch to grab hold of, although in his heart he knew it wouldn't matter. If the creature could climb, it would get him no matter how high he tried to go.

Suddenly, Sean heard a terrible howl. He looked down to see the beast tumbling off the tree trunk. The creature slammed to the ground, then ran away, whimpering.

Sean cautiously made his way back down the

tree. What had just happened? He wasn't really sure.

Sean jumped to the ground, still shaking from the fright.

This has to be a dream, Sean told himself. *I fell asleep reading the book, and now I'm dreaming.*

"Are you all right?"

Sean jumped at the sound of a voice behind him. He turned around.

The voice belonged to a small person who was just a little bit taller than Sean's knee. At least, Sean thought he was a person. His whole body, except for his face, seemed to be covered with shaggy brown hair. Small blue eyes looked brightly over a very round nose. He wore a green shirt, brown pants, and he carried a crudely made slingshot in his right hand. Sean took a step back.

"Are you going to hurt me?" he asked.

The little man looked confused at first, then looked down at his slingshot and shook his head. "I only use this to hurt exo beasts. Or enemies. You're not an enemy, are you?"

"I'm Sean," he replied. "I'm nobody's enemy. I don't even know where I am. I think it's some kind of dream."

"I am Joki," replied the man. "And I do not think you are dreaming, because that would mean that I am dreaming, too. And I am sure I woke up this morning when the mirrah bird squawked."

Sean relaxed a little bit. Joki was strange, but he seemed friendly. And he had saved Sean from the exo beast, or whatever that creature was.

"If I'm not dreaming, then maybe you can help me," Sean said. "Where am I?"

"This land is called Liasa," Joki replied.

Liasa. The land in the book *War of the Trolls.* The book's mysterious warning popped back in his mind.

Do not read this book after midnight.

But Sean had read the book after midnight. And then those strange words had appeared, and he read them, and then . . .

Sean sank to the grass as the truth sunk in. Somehow, he had been swept into the book. Now he was just another character in the story.

And he had no idea how to get out.

Joki smiled sympathetically and sat down next to Sean. He took a flask off his belt and offered it to Sean.

"Have some water," he said. "You will feel better."

Sean gratefully took a drink and handed the flask back to Joki. "Thank you," he said. "And thanks for saving me from that beast thing. I'm not from around here. I'm not even exactly sure how I got here, or how to get home."

"I knew it!" Joki jumped to his feet, his bright eyes shining with excitement. "You are human, aren't you?"

Sean nodded. "You mean you're not?"

"I am a troll," Joki said. "And you are a human. It is just like the book says."

The word "book" got Sean's attention. "What book?"

"The ancient book of my tribe," Joki answered. "It tells of a human who will have the power to help our tribe win the war against the Baka trolls. You have been sent here to lead us into battle!"

Sean didn't like the sound of that. "I'm just a kid," he said, suddenly missing his mom and dad. "I don't know anything about wars or battles. I'm not even supposed to be here. It's some kind of mistake. I just want to go home."

Joki's face softened. "Of course," he said. "You are just a boy. I was not thinking." The troll sounded terribly disappointed.

"It doesn't matter, anyway," Sean said. "I don't even know how to get home."

Joki looked thoughtful. "Perhaps the Sorceress can help you," he said. "She is not easy to find. But I can send you on your way. At least you will have a chance."

"I'll try anything," Sean said. "Just show me the way."

Joki nodded, and Sean was struck by how sad he looked. "I am sure another human will come to help us," he said. "I just hope he is not too late."

Sean hesitated. He really wanted to get home, but he hated to disappoint Joki. Maybe he was supposed to be here—maybe he was the human Joki was looking for.

After all, Sean realized, *I'm a character in a book now. Maybe this is the way the story is supposed to go.*

Sean looked at Joki. He looked small and kind of cute. If all the trolls looked that way, how bad could a troll battle be?

"Come," said Joki. "I will show you how to find the Sorceress."

If Sean decides to look for the Sorceress, go to page 22.

If Sean decides to help Joki and his tribe, go to page 27.

Continued from page 21

"Thanks," Sean said. "I think I should try to get home. I have no idea what I'm doing here."

"I can take you to the start of the path," Joki said. "But then I must get back to my people. We are getting ready to battle."

Sean followed Joki as he walked to the riverbank and then began to walk down the river, hugging the shore. He was still having a hard time believing that the whole experience was real."

"Where I come from," he explained, "Liasa isn't a real place. It's the setting of a story in a book *War of the Trolls*."

Joki turned to Sean, a look of disbelief on his face. "That cannot be."

Sean nodded. "It's true," he said. He told Joki how he had found the book, and how he had read the book after midnight, despite the warning.

The troll looked thoughtful. "Stranger things have happened in Liasa. Especially during the days of magic," he said. "Tell me, does your book say what happens when my people battle the Baka trolls?"

"I didn't get that far yet," Sean admitted. "But I hope everything works out all right."

"As do I," Joki said. He sighed.

"So tell me about the Sorceress," Sean said. "Is she, like, evil or something?"

"The Sorceress is neither good nor evil," Joki said. "During the days of magic, there was a great war among wizards and magic-users. Most destroyed one another. But the Sorceress survived. She dwells deep in the heart of Liasa, and she will help those who pass her tests. They can be quite difficult, I hear. But nobody knows for sure."

"What do you mean?" Sean asked.

Joki stopped. "Nobody who has gone to see the Sorceress has ever returned to tell the tale," he said.

"What?" Sean stopped in his tracks. He wasn't sure he wanted to see the Sorceress, after all. "You mean they all died?"

Joki shrugged. "Perhaps," he said. "Or perhaps they got what they came for. After all, if the Sorceress sends you home, I won't know, will I?"

"I guess you're right," Sean replied nervously. Suddenly, the idea of traveling to the Sorceress seemed a lot more dangerous than a battle.

"We are here," Joki said. He had stopped in front of a rickety wooden bridge that crossed the river at a narrow bend. On the other side, Sean saw a forest filled with strange-looking, colorful flowers and trees twisted into incredible shapes.

"That is the Forest of Illusion," Joki said. "Stay on the path and you will soon come to the first test of the Sorceress. What happens after that is up to you."

"Thanks," Sean said. "And thanks for saving

me before. I hope you beat those Baka trolls."

"Be careful, Sean," Joki warned. "The Sorceress is quite tricky, you know."

Joki turned and headed back up the river. Sean looked across at the unusual-looking forest and almost ran after Joki. But he took a deep breath and stepped on the bridge.

"I've got to get home," Sean said out loud. "And this is the only way. Characters in books face challenges like this all the time. If they can do it, I can do it."

Sean walked across the bridge. A heavy scent reached him before he neared the other side of the river, and he realized it came from the hundreds of flowers in the forest. It smelled spicy and sweet at the same time.

When Sean stepped off the bridge, he found a clear path leading into the woods. He started along the path.

The first thing he noticed when he entered the woods was the quiet. A blanket of silence seemed to cover the woods. Sean didn't hear a bird chirp or even a leaf rustle. His bare feet made no noise as he padded on the dirt.

Sean walked on for about fifteen minutes when the silence was broken by a cry.

"Hey, Worm!"

Sean stopped. It sounded like his brother!

"Over here!" came the voice. Sean turned to his right and saw Jake sitting in the branches of a tree.

"Jake!" Sean called up. "Did you read the book, too?"

"I'm stuck!" Jake called back. "Climb up and help me!"

Sean started to step off the path. Then he noticed something.

There was something wrong with Jake's eyes. They seemed to glimmer with a strange pink color.

Joki's words echoed in Sean's mind. *Stay on the path. The Sorceress is quite tricky.*

Sean stepped back on the path. "Is that really you?" he asked.

Jake began to laugh, and the laugh turned into a high-pitched screech. Then Jake's body transformed into a big, pink bird with a long, thin beak. The bird squawked and flew out of the tree and up toward the sky.

Sean felt scared and shaken. Seeing his brother change like that was just creepy. He turned back to the path and hurried on.

Finally, the path ended at the foot of a tall mountain. It led right into a cave. The cave looked dark inside, and Sean hesitated. But he had come this far. He bravely stepped inside.

After a few feet, he found himself inside some kind of chamber. Big hunks of pink crystal protruded from the walls, emitting a glowing light. In the light, Sean could see a tableau of tiles on the far wall of the chamber. He moved closer.

Sean studied the tiles. There were two rows of tiles arranged on top of each other. The first row was four tiles long, but the second row was missing a tile. Each of the tiles was carved with a different picture. They were arranged like this:

Tree   Feather   Flame   Drop of Water
Rock   Butterfly   Sun

Underneath the tiles, a stone table was pushed up against the wall. The table contained four loose tiles, each carved with a picture: a mountain, a cloud, a candle, and an icicle. There was a note on the table, written on white paper in pink ink.

Only one tile fits in the space above. Choose wisely, and you will continue your journey.

This must be the Sorceress's first test, Sean realized. He had to pick one of the tiles on the table to fit the missing space.

Sean studied the puzzle. The tiles must have been arranged in some kind of pattern. Once he figured out the pattern, he would know which tile to pick.

If Sean chooses the mountain, go to page 32.

If Sean chooses the cloud, go to page 56.

If Sean chooses the candle, go to page 81.

If Sean chooses the icicle, go to page 104.

Continued from page 21

Sean took a deep breath. "I'll help you," he said bravely. "I can always go to the Sorceress later."

"Thank you, thank you!" Joki gushed. "We must go to the village right away. Everyone will be so excited!"

Joki turned and hurried down a nearby path that wound through the trees. Sean followed behind him. As he kept pace with the quick little troll, thoughts raced through his mind just as quickly.

How was he going to lead the trolls in battle? He didn't know anything about battles except what he'd read in books.

Then again, he had read an awful lot of books. Maybe that made him a kind of expert, in a way. And after all, he was in a book, wasn't he? Nothing here was real. Here, he could be anyone he wanted to be—even a hero.

Sean gained confidence as he and Joki traveled through the woods. Finally, Joki stopped at the edge of the trees. Sean stopped next to him and looked down.

They were standing on top of a ridge. Below them, spread out in a valley, was the troll village. Troll-sized huts with straw roofs were neatly arranged throughout the valley. Past the huts, he could see green fields that reached the horizon.

"My village," Joki said proudly.

The troll started down a winding path that led into the valley. Sean could see more trolls—all small and hairy like Joki—begin to converge at the bottom of the trail. By the time they reached the edge, it seemed as though the whole village had turned out to greet them.

"He is human!" Joki announced to the crowd. "Just as the prophecy in the book foretells. And he has agreed to help us with our fight."

A cheer went up from the trolls. Then the crowd parted and a female troll wearing a green robe stepped up. When she reached Sean, she bowed at the waist.

"Thank you, human," she said. "Our people are grateful to you."

"I haven't done anything yet," Sean said nervously. "To tell you the truth, I'm not exactly sure what you want me to do."

The troll woman nodded. "I am Xalor," she said. "The keeper of the book. Follow me and I will tell you all you need to know."

Xalor led them to a tiny hut covered with green vines. Sean had to duck down to enter the door. He couldn't stay standing in the hut, so he sat cross-legged on the floor. Joki sat next to him.

Xalor walked to an intricately carved wooden box

and took out a thick, leather-bound book. She held up the book, and Sean gasped when he saw the title.

War of the Trolls.

"That's the book that brought me here!" he cried.

Xalor nodded. "The book brought you to us because you are the only one who can help us. Our people only desire to live here in peace. But the Baka trolls have been gathering arms for an attack. We have no way to defeat them."

She opened the book and began to read:

"The wizard handed the cube to the troll and said, "I give this helix cube to your people for their protection. If the helix cube is placed in the heart of the cave of the Baka trolls, it will destroy them. But only a human may wield it. When the time is most dire, a human will appear to save you from the Baka trolls forever."

"What's a helix cube?" Sean asked.

Xalor returned to the box and pulled out a small, solid cube that looked as though it was made out of clear crystal. A gold clasp held the lid of the cube shut.

"Only a human can open it," she said. "You must take the cube to the cave of the Baka trolls and open it before they attack us."

Sean felt relieved. All he had to do was go to a

cave and open a little box? That sounded easy.

"No problem," Sean said. "I can go right now."

Xalor nodded. "You are very brave, human," she said. She handed him the helix cube and looked at Joki. "He will need a guide."

Joki paled for a moment, then nodded. "I will go."

Xalor gave Sean a pair of shoes made of sturdy cloth, and he laced them up, grateful to have protection for his bare feet. The three stepped out of the hut and found that the villagers had all gathered around, waiting.

"Joki and the human are off to the cave of the Baka trolls," Xalor announced. "Our village is saved!"

The crowd followed Sean and Joki to the edge of the village, cheering all the way. Then Joki led Sean out of the valley into an expanse of dark woods. The cheers grew fainter as they disappeared into the trees.

They walked all afternoon. Finally, the trees began to thin out. The land looked brown and sparse compared to the green in the valley where Joki's people lived. Joki stopped behind a clump of bushes and pointed toward a tall mountain rising in the distance. Halfway up the mountain was the mouth of a large cave.

"That is the cave of the Baka trolls," he said. "Once you enter, you must follow the main path to the heart of the cave—the book says it is a small, round chamber."

Sean nodded. "I'll be right back," he said.

Sean started to step out from behind the bushes when he felt Joki pull on his pajama top. Sean knelt down next to the troll, who put a finger to his lips.

Seconds later, three huge creatures came stomping through the woods. From their hiding place, Sean had a clear view of them. Each creature was huge—three times taller than Sean. They wore animal skins over their own green-skinned bodies. They each had fingernails as long and pointy as spikes and a mouth full of hideous teeth.

Sean's heart beat wildly as the creatures passed. They walked out of the woods toward the cave.

"What were they?" Sean asked, when it was safe.

"Baka trolls," Joki replied.

Sean almost fainted. He was supposed to go into a cave filled with those monsters? All of his confidence evaporated. He wasn't a hero—he was just a regular kid!

If Sean tells Joki he can't go into the cave, go to page 44.

If Sean decides to go into the cave and face the Baka trolls, go to page 53.

Continued from page 26

"Maybe it's the mountain," Sean guessed. After all, the chamber was inside a mountain, wasn't it?

Sean picked up the tile with the picture of the mountain engraved on it. He placed it on the wall in the empty square.

The tile fit into the groove in the wall. Sean stepped back.

The floor of the chamber began to rumble. The wall with the tiles on it slid up. It wasn't a wall at all. It was a door!

Through the door, Sean could see another path, leading into a strange-looking land with a pale pink sky.

"I got it right!" he cried.

But then a rumbling sound filled the cave. A large boulder rolled down the path toward the open chamber door. Before Sean realized what was happening, the boulder slammed against the door, blocking his way.

"No way!" Sean yelled. He pounded on the boulder, but it didn't budge.

Sean leaned against the wall. The mountain must have been wrong. Now the path was blocked to him forever. He'd never get home now.

At least I'm alive, Sean told himself. From what Joki had said, a lot worse could have happened.

There was nothing to do but turn back and try to find Joki. Sean left the chamber and ran down the path, through the Forest of Illusion. Once again, the forest was quiet and still.

He had traveled about a half hour when he came to the river. Then he stopped. Something wasn't right.

Where was the bridge? It had disappeared. And the landscape around him looked different, too. Instead of lush, green woods there were dirt-covered hills dotted with a few scraggly, leafless trees.

Then, in the distance, he heard a voice.

"Help! Help!"

The sound was coming from somewhere up the river. Sean found a path leading through the scraggly trees and broke into a run. The cry sounded like a boy his own age.

The path turned sharply, and Sean found himself on top of the hill.

He gasped.

A tall tree grew on top of the hill. A large, crudely built wooden cage hung from one of the branches. Inside the cage was a boy with sandy blond hair and a vest and pants that seemed to be made of animal skins. He looked shocked to see Sean.

"Get me out of here!" the boy cried. "They'll

be back any minute!"

"What can I do?" Sean asked.

"The lock is on top of the cage," the boy answered. "Can you climb?"

"Sure," Sean said. He shimmied up the tree and crawled out onto the branch from which the cage dangled. On top of the cage, there was a flat piece of wood slid into a bracket of some kind. Sean reached out and slid the wood back. Then he opened the lid of the cage.

The boy inside didn't hesitate. He scrambled up through the top of the cage.

"We've got to hurry," he said.

Sean didn't question him. He started back down the tree. The boy followed him. When the boy's feet touched the ground, he looked back and forth.

"Follow me," he said.

The boy started to run down the hill. Sean ran behind him. He had so many questions he wanted to ask, but the boy seemed to think getting out of the area was urgent.

Then Sean realized why.

A huge creature was stomping toward them up the hill. He looked sort of human, but he was as tall as the tree on the hill, and his skin was a sickly green. Huge muscles bulged on his arms and legs. Large, crooked teeth stuck out of his drooling mouth. He wore spiked leather bracelets on each wrist and a fur garment that draped over his shoulders and reached down below his waist. When he saw the boys, he let out a hideous cry.

The boy stopped abruptly, and a look of pure fear swept across his face.

"What should we do?" Sean asked.

If the boys run down the hill and past the troll, go to page 42.

If the boys run back up the hill, go to page 64.

Continued from page 69

"Let's go to the Cave of Transformation," Sean urged. "We can do this."

Taran nodded. "You are right. Let's go."

"I'll take the book," Sean said, tucking it under his arm.

"The elders will not like that," Taran worried.

"The elders won't know until we're gone," Sean pointed out. "So let's get going."

The boys left the chambers and made their way through the village. All was quiet, and only a few of the cabins had lights in their windows.

Taran led Sean out of the village, and Sean noticed they were heading for the hills. Once they were away from the cabins, Taran spoke.

"The Cave of Transformation is legendary," Taran said. "I know it is somewhere in the hills. It is supposed to be near the Weeping Trees."

"Where are they?" Sean asked.

Taran shrugged. "I do not know," he said. "But we can look."

They walked in silence for a while, and Sean had a chance to organize his thoughts. He knew he wasn't dreaming, that was for sure. Everything felt too real. He was in Liasa, the land that was the setting of the book *War of the Trolls*. Somehow, he had entered the story. And he had no idea how to get home.

The magic gem might help, if they could find it. In books, magic gems always had cool powers. Of course, the gem might also help the villagers take on the attacking trolls. Sean knew he had to get home soon. The thought of his family worrying about where he was made him sad. But it also made him sad to think of Taran and all those villagers being attacked by the trolls.

We need to find the stone first, Sean told himself. *Then I'll worry about what to do next.*

Finally, they arrived at the hills. Taran stopped.

"The Weeping Trees should be near here," he said. "But I don't know what they look like."

The boys walked around the hillside from tree to tree. All the trees looked normal. Sean was examining a tree trunk when he heard Taran call.

"This is hopeless!" he cried. "We will never find it."

Sean looked up. Taran was leaning against a tree trunk. The tree Taran rested on was curved sharply to the right, and its branches almost swept the ground. To the right of the tree was another tree exactly like it. This tree's trunk curved to the left, as though it was reaching for the other tree.

Like they are sad, Sean realized. *Or weeping.*

"Taran, come here!" Sean called back. He saw that the space between the branches of the two trees formed a perfect archway. And through the archway, in the distance, Sean could see a large boulder. He pointed it out to Taran.

"It looks like the trees are sad," he said. "And like they're leading the way to that rock."

The boys slowly walked toward the boulder. As they neared it, Sean saw that some kind of writing had been engraved on it. When he got close enough, he read the words aloud:

Enter Here the Cave of Transformation

Step Lightly But Wisely

"But how do we get in?" Taran asked. As Taran spoke, the book slipped out of Sean's arms and fell to the ground. It spilled open. Sean picked it up, but before he closed it, he noticed something. The words on the page were about the cave!

"Go to the Cave of Transformation," the wizard told him. "When you arrive, knock on the stone three times, and the cave will be opened to you."

Sean couldn't believe it. It was as though the book knew what was happening and was trying to help them. "I think I know what to do," he said. He closed the book, keeping his finger on the page so he wouldn't lose his place. Then he knocked on the stone three times.

The boulder slid to the side, revealing a small chamber. Glowing stones placed on pillars around the room lit the space with an eerie green light. Sean could see that the floor was made up of flat stones inscribed with pictures and symbols. He could make out an owl, a rose, a bolt of lightning, a horse, and other images.

Sean started to walk inside, but Taran stopped him. "What does it mean—step lightly but wisely?" Taran asked.

Sean thought. "Maybe it's just advice," he said. "Or maybe we have to be careful where we step."

Sean studied the pictures. "Maybe we should step on the rose first," he said. "Roses are pretty flowers. That's got to be safe, right?"

Taran nodded. The boys looked at each other and then stepped on the stone together.

Behind them, the boulder slid shut, blocking off the entrance. In the next instant, sharp spikes emerged from the walls on either side of them. A groaning sound filled the chamber as the walls began to close in on them.

Then it hit Sean—the spikes looked just like thorns! "We stepped on the wrong stone," he said, trying to keep calm. "Maybe if we step on another stone, the walls will stop moving."

"Which one?" Taran asked.

If Sean and Taran step on the square engraved with a horse, go to page 74.

If the boys step on the square engraved with an owl, go to page 77.

Sean looked at the key, then at the doors.

Then he got it.

It was just like the first challenge. The images on the doors represented the four elements. The garden was Earth. The blowing leaves were Air. The volcano was Fire. The river was Water.

The bird on the key had to represent air. That meant the second door had to be the way home.

Sean hoped he was right. He put the key in the second door and turned it.

The door swung open. Sean found himself back in his bedroom. Morning light streamed through the window.

Sean sat on his bed, stunned. Had he really been to Liasa? The whole experience was too bizarre to be true.

He spotted *War of the Trolls* open on his bed and grabbed it. He hadn't finished reading it last night. Now that he had actually been in Liasa, he wanted to know more.

Before he could start, Jake burst through his door.

"Hey, Worm," he said. "Mom wants to go hiking today. She wants to know if you want to come."

Sean started to say that he wanted to stay home and read. Then he stopped. He had tried hard to get home. Now that he was here, he realized he wanted to spend some time with his family.

Besides, before he would have hated the idea of hiking. He'd have thought it would be too hard. But in Liasa, he had done a lot of things he thought he would never do.

Sean put the book down on his bed.

"I'll go," he said. "Just let me get changed."

THE END

Continued from page 16 and page 35

The boy didn't answer. He seemed to be frozen in fear.

Sean grabbed him by the arm. "Keep running!" he cried. Sean continued speeding down the hill, practically dragging the boy behind him.

Sean cut a wide path to the right, trying to avoid the creature. He couldn't see the bottom of the hill yet, but he hoped there was some way of avoiding the creature once they got there.

But the creature was surprisingly fast for his size. He stomped across the ground toward the boys and scooped up one in each hand.

Sean gagged as a rotting smell reached his nostrils. The creature's damp, sweaty hand enclosed him in a tight grip. He kicked and struggled, but he couldn't break free. In the other hand, the boy looked limp and defeated.

The creature plodded up the hill and dropped them both through the open top of the cage. Sean landed on the hard floor with a thud. He heard the cage lid close shut.

The creature stuck his huge, hideous face up to the bars.

"Eat soon," he growled. Then he stomped over to a nearby rock and sat down, his arms folded.

"What is going on?" Sean asked. "What is that thing?"

"It's a troll," the boy answered in a flat voice.

A troll? Sean thought incredulously. "Is this—is this Liasa?" Sean asked.

The boy nodded.

Sean jumped to his feet. "Cool! I'm in the book!" he cried. He turned to the boy. "So what happens now? Will someone come rescue us?"

The boy sadly shook his head. "No," he said. "My people put me here. They send one of us to the trolls every seven years."

Sean didn't like the sound of that. "For what?" he asked.

"You heard the troll," he said. "They're going to eat us."

An icy chill crept over Sean's body. "No way," he said, his voice rising. "This isn't real! This isn't real!"

Sean shook the bars of the cage. "I want to go back! Get me out of the book!"

The boy looked up at Sean with defeated eyes. "There's no way out," he said. "We'll be troll food soon. There's nothing we can do."

"Nooooooo!" Sean cried.

THE END

Continued from page 31

Sean turned to Joki. "I don't think I can do this," he said. "I thought the trolls would be more like . . . well, like you."

Joki looked solemn. "Baka trolls are quite fierce. Few of my people have been brave enough to face them. I would not blame you if you do not want to go."

Sean looked at the retreating Baka trolls. They were huge monsters! He had no idea how to get past them. He didn't have any weapons or magical tools or any training, for that matter. He was just a kid who liked to read.

"I don't think I'm the human in your prophecy," he said. "You need someone who can do stuff. A hero. I'm just a kid."

Joki nodded, and Sean could tell he was masking disappointment. "Let us go, then," he said. "It will be dark soon."

The two headed back into the woods, and they walked back to the troll village in silence. The sun had set by the time they arrived, and they found the villagers scurrying around, preparing for battle. But when they saw Joki and Sean, they gathered around with hopeful looks on their faces.

"The Baka trolls still live," Joki announced. "We must ready ourselves for the attack."

A murmur went up among the trolls, but no one confronted Sean. Xalor walked up and gave him a kind look.

"Facing the Baka trolls is no task for a child," she said, taking the helix cube from him. "At least you tried. We are grateful for that."

Xalor turned and walked away. Sean felt terrible. The trolls were so nice! He thought of the Baka trolls attacking them and shuddered.

"You must be tired, Sean," Joki said. "Let me take you to my cabin. You should rest."

The thought of spending the night somewhere else besides his own bed startled Sean. "I guess I should try to find that Sorceress tomorrow so I can get back home."

Joki gazed out at the villagers. "If there is a tomorrow," he murmured.

Sean followed Joki through the village until they came to a small hut with a neat bed of flowers planted next to the front door.

"I am sure my bed is too small for you, but the floor is clean," he said. "Get a good sleep." Then he turned away.

"Where are you going?" Sean asked.

Joki turned around. "To help prepare for battle. We need all the hands we can to defeat the Bakas."

"I want to help," Sean blurted out, surprising himself.

Joki's eyes narrowed. "You said so yourself. You are not a hero."

"I know," Sean said. "But I can't just sit here while you guys fight. I mean, I was scared to go into the cave. But I want to still help if I can."

Joki nodded. "We must find you a weapon."

Joki led Sean to a long, low building on the outskirts of the village.

"Our people do not have much use for weapons," he said. "But we keep them in case we need them."

Joki opened the door, and Sean saw that the building was crammed with all kinds of battle gear. Trolls filled the floor, trying on vests and helmets and picking up swords.

"First, protection," Joki said. He walked over to a pile of leather vests and sorted through them. Finally, he pulled one out.

"This looks like the biggest."

Sean slipped the vest over his shoulders. The bottom didn't even reach his belly button. But it was better than nothing.

Joki found him a leather helmet next. The flaps barely reached the tops of his ears. Sean knew he must look ridiculous.

"Now you need a weapon," Joki said. He took the slingshot off his belt. "I could find you a slingshot. I'll teach you how to use it. They are very effective. But you may choose something else if you like."

Sean looked at the weapon and imagined hitting one of the giant Baka trolls with a tiny rock. The thought didn't make him feel very safe.

Sean looked around the room. Some of the trolls were swinging stubby swords made of grimy metal. He saw one sword mounted on the opposite wall.

"What about a sword?" he asked.

Joki frowned and scurried toward the sword. "That is a magic sword," he said. "Flimsy metal. Quite useless unless you study the inscriptions on the handle. Then it is quite powerful."

Sean liked the sound of the magical sword. He wasn't a fighter, really. He was a good reader. He might be able to figure out the inscriptions.

But Joki had said the sword would be useless if he didn't figure out the inscriptions. Maybe he was better off learning how to use a slingshot.

If Sean chooses the magic sword, go to page 135.

If Sean chooses a slingshot, go to page 48.

"I guess I'll take a slingshot," Sean said. "As long as you teach me how to use it."

Joki nodded. "We should have time. And I could use the practice myself."

Joki grabbed a slingshot for Sean and picked up a cloth sack and filled it with rocks. "Let's go to the fields," he said.

Although it was dark, the fields were lit by torches planted in the ground. Other trolls were practicing using their slingshots, aiming rocks at pumpkin-like vegetables positioned on the wooden fence that surrounded the fields.

"Baka trolls are big," Joki explained. "But they are slow. And they do have a weak spot."

Joki stood on his toes, reached up, and touched the spot right between Sean's eyes.

"One hit there, and even the biggest Baka troll will go down," Joki said. "It just takes practice."

He handed the slingshot to Sean, who looked at it doubtfully. But it was worth a try.

Joki aimed at a pumpkin, pulled back the band, released it, and a stone went flying.

Whap! The pumpkin exploded.

"Now you try," Joki said.

On Sean's first attempt, the stone didn't go more than three feet. But he kept on. *Whap!*

Whap! Whap! Before long, he was smashing pumpkins with the rest of the trolls.

"You are a natural, Sean," Joki said, smiling.

"Thanks," Sean said proudly. Besides reading, he didn't think he was good at anything else. But he felt like a pro with the slingshot.

Suddenly, a loud horn rang. Joki tensed.

"The Bakas are approaching," he said. "We must take our places."

Joki and Sean each filled a sack with stones. Then they headed to the northern border of the village, near the forest that led to the Baka cave. Xalor was yelling instructions to the trolls.

"Slingshots in the trees!" she cried. "Swords on the ground! The Bakas are not used to being counterattacked. But we will stand firm!"

The trolls let out a cheer, and then the slingshot-bearers headed for the trees. Sean ran alongside Joki, until he came to an oak tree that looked good for climbing. He shimmied up and found a comfortable spot between two thick branches.

As soon as he was settled, the tree trunk began to shake. All the trees seemed to be shaking.

Then the Baka trolls emerged from the trees. Sean felt frozen with fright as the huge monsters stomped toward the village. They each carried large wooden clubs studded with spikes.

"Fire!" Xalor cried. Before Sean could even

load his slingshot, he heard a stone whizzing past his tree. The stone hit the lead Baka troll right between the eyes, and the Baka fell with a thud.

The other Bakas roared angrily. One ran up to a tree and began shaking it. To Sean's horror, he saw a troll fall from the branches. It was Joki!

Sean acted quickly. He loaded his slingshot, aimed it at the Baka, and sent the stone flying.

He hit it! The Baka crashed to the ground.

Joki scrambled to his feet, climbed back up the tree and waved to Sean. "Thank you!" he cried.

Sean felt a surge of pride. He set his sights on the other Baka trolls. There seemed to be an endless army of them pouring out of the trees.

Sean took a deep breath and focused. *Whap! Whap! Whap!* He shot stone after stone. He had taken down his seventeenth Baka troll when he reached into his bag and found it empty.

He thought about climbing down to get more stones when he heard a loud cry come from the Bakas. He froze. Were more coming?

But the Baka trolls were retreating. They stomped back up the trail, dragging their fallen comrades behind them. A cheer went up.

Sean climbed down the tree. He found Joki waiting for him.

"We did it!" Joki cried. "The Baka trolls are not used to resistance. They will set their sights on another village now."

"That's great!" Sean cried.

"And I must thank you, for saving me," Joki said.

"You saved me first, remember?"

The trolls gathered in the center of the village for a celebration. Sean felt happy to have helped the trolls. But he was starting to miss his family.

"Maybe you should tell me how to find that Sorceress," Sean told Joki. "I think I should try to get home."

Xalor overheard him. "The path to the Sorceress is far too dangerous," she said. "But I believe the helix cube may help you get home."

"The helix cube? How?" Sean asked.

"The texts are unclear," Xalor said. "They were translated from an ancient language. The cube must be opened at a crossroads either at the break of day or the start of night. I am not sure which."

"Couldn't I try both?" Sean asked.

"You could," Xalor replied. "But if you are wrong, I cannot tell what may happen. Make your choice carefully."

If Sean uses the helix cube at the break of day, go to page 58.

If Sean uses the helix cube at the start of night, go to page 111.

Continued from page 121

Sean thought the color of the keys might be the answer. The key was gold, and so was the sun.

Sean took the gold key from his hook. He put the key in the lock of the door and turned it.

A cloud of darkness immediately fell over him. Sean got a sick feeling in his stomach, as though the ground beneath his feet was being ripped away from him. Then the light returned. But Sean was no longer standing at the stone wall. He was back in the Forest of Illusion.

"*Squaaawk!*"

Sean looked up to see the pink bird perched in a nearby tree branch. The bird shook its head at Sean.

"You lose!" the bird squawked. "Too bad. You got pretty far."

"Wait!" Sean yelled. "Take me back! I'll get it right this time."

But the bird flew away.

Sean looked around. He wasn't on the path he had taken before. He was surrounded by the strange-looking flowers and trees of the forest, and he had no idea where to go or what to do.

"Help!" Sean yelled. "Anybody out there?"

But nobody answered.

THE END

Continued from page 31

"Sean, are you all right?" Joki asked.

Sean didn't answer right away. He wasn't sure what to do. He definitely didn't want to go anywhere near that cave.

Then he remembered the hopeful faces of the cheering trolls in the village. He couldn't let them down.

"I'm fine," he said. "Let's get this over with."

Joki looked relieved. "If you're sure."

"I'm sure," Sean said, although he really wasn't. "Just give a yell if you see any more Bakas coming, okay?"

Joki nodded. "The entrance is never guarded," he said. "The Bakas know that no one is brave enough to enter. Until now."

That made Sean feel a little better. If the cave wasn't guarded, he might be able to slip in and open the helix box before any of the trolls saw him. Sean stepped out from behind the bushes and looked up at the mountain. The Baka trolls had already entered the cave.

Sean walked to the foot of the mountain and started up the rocky trail that led to the mouth of the cave. Before he entered, he cautiously peeked inside. But all he could see was blackness.

For a second, Sean thought about turning

back. But he steeled himself. He took a deep breath and stepped through the mouth of the cave. He could barely see in the dim light, but he just kept moving on the path as Joki had said.

He followed the twisting and turning path for a few minutes. To his surprise, he saw a small doorway lit by torches. The doorway bore an inscription in English:

THE PORTAL OF TIME AND DIMENSION.

Sean's heart beat quickly. This could be a way home! He almost stepped inside, then remembered the helix cube in his hand.

He had a job to do. He could destroy the Baka trolls, then use the portal to get home.

Sean continued down the path. It curved sharply to the right, and he turned the corner . . .

And bumped right into a Baka troll!

The huge troll looked confused for a second. Then his bloodshot eyes looked down and spotted Sean. He swiped at Sean with his meaty fist.

"HUMAN!" The troll's cry echoed through the cave. Sean ran through the troll's legs, but the Baka turned quickly and grabbed Sean by the leg. The helix cube tumbled out of Sean's hands and disappeared into a dark corner.

The troll held Sean by the ankle, dangling him upside down above the cave floor. He stomped ahead down the path.

"I take you to leader, human," the troll said.

They went a few feet until they came to a round chamber. Pathways led out of the chamber like the rays of the sun. Sean realized it must be the heart of the cave that Joki had told him about.

Sean tried to think. There was no way out of the troll's grip. Unless . . .

With all of his strength, Sean reached up and yanked at the lace on the shoe. He slipped out and landed with a thud on the ground.

But the dense Baka troll didn't notice. He kept stomping down the path, holding Sean's shoe.

Sean knew he didn't have much time. He raced back down the pathway.

At least I tried, he told himself. *I didn't give up.*

As he ran, a glittering object caught his eye. Sean stopped short. The helix cube!

Sean didn't know what to do. He could grab the cube and run back to the heart of the cave and hope he didn't get caught again. Or he could just head right for the Portal of Time and Dimension and try to get home safe and sound— before things got any worse.

If Sean goes to the Portal of Time and Dimension, go to page 70.

If Sean takes the helix cube to the heart of the cave, go to page 93.

Continued from page 26

Sean studied the bottom row of tiles. *Rock. Butterfly. Sun.*

He looked at the tiles on the table again. *Mountain. Cloud. Candle. Icicle.* None of the choices jumped out at him.

Choose carefully, the note had warned. But Sean had to choose something, or he'd never get home.

"It's got to be the cloud," he finally guessed out loud. "Clouds go with sun, right?"

There was no answer to his question, but Sean hadn't really thought there would be. He picked up the tile with the picture of the cloud on it and placed it into the empty space on the wall. A groove in the wall held the tile in place. Sean stepped back.

The chamber began to rumble. Sean felt something hit the top of his head. He looked up to see the ceiling of the chamber sliding open, sending dust and pebbles scattering into the chamber below.

The ceiling opened to reveal a pale pink sky. Sean held his breath. Was this the way to the next challenge? If so, then how was he supposed to climb up there?

"Squaaaaaaaaawk!"

A high-pitched screech filled the air. A shadow

filled the chamber. In the next instant, a big pink bird swooped down from the sky. It latched onto Sean's pajama top with its claws.

"Hey!" Sean yelled.

The bird only screeched in reply. It flew up and out of the chamber. Sean struggled to free himself, but soon they were too high. They soared across the pink sky, over a lake filled with pink water.

Maybe this is the way to the second challenge, Sean told himself. *It has to be, right?*

"*Squaaaaawk!*"

Then the bird let go . . .

THE END

Continued from page 51

Sean thought carefully. Break of day or start of night. He tried to think like a character in a book.

In books, nighttime was usually a good time for magic. That would be one reason to open the cube at the start of night.

But scary things happened at night too. And Xalor had said that something might go wrong if he opened the box at the wrong time . . .

"I'll wait until dawn," Sean decided.

Xalor nodded. "It could be risky," she said. "You know you are welcome to live here with us if you like."

Sean looked around the village. The trolls looked happy, and their huts looked cheerful. It wouldn't be a bad place to live—better than Bleaktown, anyway. But he knew he would miss his family too much.

"Thanks," he said. "But I've got to try. No matter what happens."

The trolls' celebration lasted through most of the night. Sean ate and danced with the trolls until late, then fell asleep on a soft mat on Joki's floor. He awoke to find the troll shaking his shoulders.

"It's time, Sean," Joki said.

Sean sat up and rubbed his eyes. Joki and the trolls had been so nice. He would miss them. But he couldn't stay in Liasa forever.

Joki led Sean to the middle of the village, where the trolls were gathered around the crossroads, where the two main paths met. Xalor waited at the head of the group, holding the helix cube.

"Good luck," she said.

"What do I need to do?" Sean asked.

"Just stand in the center of the crossroads and open the box," she replied. "If the time is right, the box will take you back home."

Sean nodded and took the box from Xalor. He walked into the crossroads and looked down at the cube.

A silver clasp closed the lid of the silver box. Sean looked up one last time.

"Good-bye," he said.

Joki waved. Sean looked back down at the cube and opened the clasp.

A bright light shot out of the box, blinding him. Then Sean's body went limp. The light picked him up and whirled him around. He felt like he was in some kind of mystical tornado.

Then everything stopped. Sean blinked.

He wasn't home, that was for sure. He was in some kind of room with white walls. There didn't seem to be any doors or windows.

"Hello?" Sean called out.

Outside the room, he heard noises. They were

deep and muffled, but he could make out Joki's voice.

"Did he get home?"

"I hope so." That was Xalor talking. "Let us return the cube to its place."

Sean suddenly felt the room move, and he tumbled on his side.

That's when he realized the truth.

He was *inside* the cube. He must have opened the cube at the wrong time.

Sean jumped to his feet and pounded on the walls.

"Help!" he yelled. "It's me! Sean! I'm in here!"

Xalor and Joki didn't answer. Sean kept pounding.

They had to hear him. Xalor had to find a way to get him out.

It was his only hope.

THE END

Continued from page 121

At first, Sean thought the riddle was about the color of the keys. The sun was gold. But he wasn't sure what color an owl's eyes were or what currants looked like.

He thought about the shapes on top of the keys. The sun, an owl's eye, and a pie were all round! The key topped with a circle had to be the right choice.

Sean took the silver key off its hook. He placed it in the lock and turned it.

The door swung open. Sean looked inside. Behind the stone wall grew a garden overrun with vines and flowers. All the flowers were different shades of pink, although they were different shapes and sizes. In the center of the garden was a tall tree. Frilly pink flowers bloomed among its pale green leaves.

Sean stepped into the garden. He heard a creak and looked back to see the door slam shut behind him. He turned back and looked around for any sign of a challenge or even the Sorceress.

"Hello?" Sean called out.

In response, a huge spider dropped down from the tree on a thin strand of webbing. The spider was the size of a small dog. Black fur covered its body and its eight dangling legs. On top of its head was a mass of bright pink eyeballs. Two sharp ivory fangs stuck out of its slim mouth.

"*Aaaaaah!*" Sean screamed and ran back toward the door. He pulled and pulled, but the door wouldn't open.

"You have tried so hard to get here," said a smooth voice behind him. "Why do you want to leave now?"

Sean turned and realized it was the spider talking.

Why not? he thought. *I had a conversation with a fish, after all.*

"It's just that, uh . . . you scared me," Sean said. "You're not going to hurt me?"

The spider made a squeaky sound that resembled a laugh. "That is not my purpose," she said. "My purpose is to challenge you."

"Another challenge?" Sean wasn't sure he could handle one more.

"The Sorceress does not grant favors lightly," answered the spider. "Those who seek her must be worthy."

Sean nodded, determined not to fail. He had come so far, and this Sorceress was his only way home.

"What's the challenge?" Sean asked.

The spider's eyes focused on Sean. "You have a way with words," she said. "But are you as good with numbers as well?"

Sean didn't answer. Math wasn't his greatest subject. It was probably because he spent his homework time reading books instead of studying.

The spider seemed to read his mind. "Then this will be a good challenge," she said. "Listen carefully:

This number is more than the number of my legs.

But less than the number you get if you add my brother's legs.

It can't be divided evenly by two or three.

And it's closer to fifteen than ten."

Sean was furiously counting in his head as the spider chanted. "Can you repeat that?" he asked.

"Of course not," said the spider. "Then it wouldn't be a challenge."

Sean took a deep breath. He thought he knew the number.

If Sean says the number is fourteen, go to page 72.

If Sean says the number is thirteen, go to page 76.

Continued from page 16 and page 35

The boy seemed frozen to the spot. Sean grabbed his arm and shook him.

"Come on!" Sean cried.

The boy snapped back to reality. "They hate water," he said. "We've got to get to the river."

The creature stomped after them, incredibly fast for his size. Then the path ended, and the boy splashed into the river. Sean jumped in and pushed off as hard as he could, breaking into a swim. He didn't look back until he was halfway across.

The troll stood on the shore. The boy stopped swimming and called back to Sean.

"He won't follow us in!" he yelled. "Keep swimming!"

Sean didn't argue. His limbs ached, but he kept swimming. Soon the river forked, and the boy swam to the left. Sean followed. They hadn't gone far when the boy climbed up on the riverbank.

"We got away," he said in a tone that revealed he didn't quite believe it.

"What was that thing?" Sean asked.

The boy looked at him quizzically. "A troll!" he answered. "Are you feeling all right?"

"I'm not really from around here," Sean answered. "Where is here, anyway?"

"The River of Sorrow," said the boy.

"I mean, what's the name of the whole place?" Sean asked. "Is this anywhere near Bleaktown?"

"Our land is called Liasa," the boy said, looking more and more suspicious. "I am Taran."

Liasa. The land inside the book. Did that mean . . .

Sean couldn't accept the thought. He couldn't be in the book, could he? That was impossible.

"I need to find a way home," Sean said. "Is there a telephone around here?"

"I do not know what you mean," said Taran. "I am sure someone in my village can help you, as you helped me. Although I am not sure they will welcome us." His face grew dark.

"Why not?" Sean asked. "And why were you stuck in that cage, anyway?"

Taran stood. "Let us talk as we travel."

Sean nodded and got to his feet. Taran led him away from the river. They walked among the trees in silence for a while. Then Taran spoke.

"The trolls cause destruction all over Liasa," said Taran. "But my village made an agreement with them. Every seven years, one of the villagers is sent to the trolls."

Sean suddenly felt queasy. "For food," he said.

"Yes," Taran said, avoiding his eyes. "For food. This year, I was chosen."

"But you got away. Won't the people in your

village be happy about that?" Sean asked.

"Not at all," Taran answered. "The pact has been broken. Now the trolls will attack. No one in the village will be safe."

Sean stopped. "So why are we going there? Maybe you should run away to somewhere safe."

Taran shook his head. "I must warn my people."

After about a half hour, the village came into sight. The woods ended, and a collection of small, wooden cabins came into view. To the right stretched a green field planted with crops.

Men, women, and children dressed in animal skins walked among the cabins, talking, playing, carrying water, or performing other daily tasks. As Sean and Taran grew closer, the people slowly began to stop what they were doing. Soon a hush of silence fell over the crowd. They stared at Taran as though they were seeing a ghost.

Sean waited for Taran to say something. But a man with a long, white beard pushed through the crowd and spoke first.

"Taran," he said gravely. "What have you done?"

Taran stood firm. "I escaped, Ozar," he said.

The man's expression grew grim. "This will be dealt with harshly, Taran. You know the consequences of your actions."

Another man pushed through the crowd. He also had a long, white beard. But he was taller and thinner, and Sean thought his dark eyes looked a little bit kinder than Ozar's cold blue ones.

"Let us bring them to the chambers," he said. "This is a matter for all of the elders."

Ozar nodded. "Yes, Malchior," he said.

Taran and Sean followed the bearded men through the village, past the villagers, who looked at them with trepidation. They entered a low building. Inside was a long, wooden table surrounded by chairs. Ozar sat at the head of the table. Malchior motioned to two chairs in a corner.

"Be still until we call on you," he said sternly.

In the next few minutes, more villagers entered the room. The men all had long, white beards. The women had white hair worn in long braids. Soon twelve elders sat around the table.

"Taran, rise," Malchior said. "Tell us your story."

So Taran explained how Sean had arrived and helped him escape from the cage.

Malchior looked at Sean curiously. "And where are you from?" he asked.

"Bleaktown," Sean answered.

Malchior frowned. "There is something not right about this boy," he said.

"That is the least of our troubles," Ozar said. He stood and walked to a corner of the room, where a large book was perched on a pedestal. "The trolls will attack soon. We must find a way to defeat them."

Ozar held up the book. "The answer is here, if only we can decipher it."

One of the elders snorted. "No one has been able to decipher the book. You know that, Ozar."

A ray of sunlight shone through a window, illuminating the book's title *War of the Trolls*.

Sean gasped. "I can read it!" he cried.

The elders cried out in surprise. Ozar's face grew red. "The boy lies! It is impossible that one of his age can read the ancient text."

"Take the boys away while we discuss this further."

The elder led the boys to a small cabin. Taran was quiet, and Sean had time to think. *The War of the Trolls* book had most likely brought him here. Maybe it could get him home, too. He had to get his hands on it.

Through the window, he could see the sun setting. Finally, Malchior came to see them.

"We have more to discuss," he said. "You will be called back to the chambers in the morning. I suggest you sleep well."

Malchior left, and Sean turned to Taran. "I wasn't lying," he said. "I can read that book. Let's go back to the chambers, and I'll prove it to you."

Taran looked worried. "It would be dangerous," he said.

"You said the trolls will attack the village. *That's* dangerous," Sean pointed out. "Maybe I can find something in the book that will help."

Taran nodded. "Let's try," he said.

The boys snuck out of the cabin and quietly made their way to the elders' chambers. Taran peeked in the window and saw that the room was empty. He and Sean crept inside.

Sean took the book to a window. A shaft of moonlight illuminated the pages.

Sean leafed through the book, looking for a way back home or for more information about the trolls. Finally, he found it.

"Look here," he said. "The book says something about a gem with magic powers. It's in something called the Cave of Transformation."

Taran's eyes shone. "I have heard of that!"

"We can go there," Sean said. "We can use the stone to defeat the trolls." *And maybe send me back home*, he added silently to himself.

"We must tell Malchior," Taran said. "He is fair and wise. The elders should know about this."

Sean wasn't so sure. Malchior didn't seem so bad, but he was still an elder. "Maybe we should go by ourselves," Sean said. "If the elders try to stop us, there'll be no hope."

If Sean and Taran ask Malchior for help, go to page 88.

If Sean and Taran try to search for the gem on their own, go to page 36.

Continued from page 55

Sean couldn't stand the idea of facing the Baka troll again. He left the helix cube where it was and raced down the path until he came to the doorway of the Portal of Time and Dimension.

Sean quickly checked the outside of the doorway. There were no instructions. He wasn't even sure if the portal could take him home.

Before he could step inside, a thunderous cry roared through the tunnel.

"HUMAN!"

The Baka troll turned the corner and charged toward Sean, fuming. Slimy drool dripped from his sharp fangs.

Sean ran inside the doorway into the pitch-black portal. The air inside crackled with electricity. Sean twirled around. What was he supposed to do?

The Baka troll stuck his head inside the portal.

"HUMAN!" he growled again.

Sean panicked. "I want to go home!" he cried. "I want to go home now!"

A tunnel of purple light swirled through the portal. Sean's skin tingled, and he suddenly felt dizzy.

Then the light stopped swirling. Sean blinked.

He was back in his bedroom. Outside the window, stars shone in the night sky. The book

War of the Trolls was open on his bed, just as he had left it.

"It worked!" Sean said happily.

He sat on the bed, relieved. He couldn't believe everything he had been through. Fighting off a two-headed beast. Meeting a tribe of trolls. Escaping from a hideous Baka troll.

But now he was home, safe.

Then his bedroom floor began to shake.

A wave of fear swept over Sean. Something was coming down the hallway toward him. Something big enough to make the floor vibrate with every massive step.

The Baka troll stuck his head through Sean's bedroom doorway. It burst into the room and lunged at Sean.

"HUMAN!"

THE END

Continued from page 63

Sean tried to remember the spider's words. He knew the number was between eight and sixteen. And it was closer to fifteen than ten . . .

"Is it fourteen?" Sean asked.

The spider's eyes flashed.

"I am sorry," she said.

Without warning, a sticky strand of webbing shot out from the spider. It wrapped around Sean like a snake. Then the spider began to pull Sean forward.

"Hey!" Sean cried. He struggled to break free, but the webbing was too strong.

As the spider pulled Sean closer, she shot out more and more webbing. The strand wrapped around Sean until every part of his body except for his head was wound in the web.

The spider grasped the webbing with her legs and pulled Sean close to her head. He saw his reflection in all of her eyes.

Then he fainted.

When Sean came to, the spider's puzzle was chanting in his head. He realized, too late, the line he had forgotten.

It can't be divided evenly by two or three.

Fourteen could be divided evenly by two. That meant the right answer was thirteen.

"I know the answer!" Sean cried. "It's thirteen!"

The spider swung next to Sean. At first, he thought the spider was upside down, but then he realized it was him. He was hanging upside down from the tree branch.

"Your answer comes too late," she said. "It's a pity, really."

"What are you going to do with me?" Sean asked.

"Don't worry, Sean," the spider replied. "It won't hurt a bit."

The spider sank her fangs through the webbed cocoon and into Sean's leg. It stung for a minute, and then Sean felt pleasantly sleepy.

"What's . . . happening?" Sean asked.

"I may set you free," said the spider. "Then again, I may eat you. I haven't decided yet. Until then, sleep."

Sean fought to stay awake, but he couldn't. As he drifted off to sleep, one thought screamed in his mind:

Please don't eat me!

THE END

Continued from page 39

As the walls inched closer to them, Sean tried to think of what to do. In most of the fantasy books he had read, the main character usually had to figure out puzzles or riddles along the way. Maybe the Cave of Transformation was a puzzle.

Sean looked at the tiles again. An owl, a bolt of lightning, a horse . . .

"Sean, we need to do something fast!" Taran cried.

Fast . . . that was it! A horse was fast. Maybe if they stepped on the horse, they would escape the spikes.

"Let's step on the horse," Sean suggested.

Taran nodded, and the boys stepped on the horse tile at the same time. The walls stopped moving.

"Whew, that was close," Sean said. The sharp spikes were grazing his skin.

The tile suddenly sank underneath their feet, and the boys plummeted through a hole in the floor. Sean lost his footing and found himself sliding down a long, stone slide.

The slide twisted and turned and seemed to go on forever. Finally, it stopped, and the boys tumbled onto the hard stone ground.

"Where are we?" Taran asked, rising to his

feet. "Have we found the stone?"

Sean stood up and looked around. They were in another chamber. This one was empty, except for a stone horse's head that protruded from the wall. Its two eyes were made of sparkling blue gems that gave the chamber a faint glow.

"I'm not sure," Sean said. He opened the book and found the section about the cave again. Then he turned the page and read:

When you enter the Cave of Transformation, step on the tile engraved with an owl—certainly a wise choice. All other choices lead to disaster. Those who step on the rose will be felled by sharp spikes. Those who step on the horse will be swiftly transported to an underground chamber from which there is no return.

Sean's stomach flip-flopped. *No return.*

"What does it say?" Taran asked.

Sean sat down under the glowing light of the horse's eyes. There had to be a way out of the chamber. He'd read every word of the book. He'd have to find something.

After all, Sean thought bitterly. *I've got plenty of time to read now.*

THE END

Sean went over the challenge in his head.

This number is more than the number of my legs. But less than the number you get if you add my brother's legs. A spider had eight legs, so the number had to be more than eight and less than sixteen.

It can't be divided evenly by two or three. The numbers nine, ten, twelve, fourteen, and fifteen could all be divided evenly by two and three. That meant the number had to be eleven or thirteen.

And it's closer to fifteen than ten. The answer had to be thirteen!

"Is it thirteen?" Sean asked.

A bright pink light glowed from the spider's eyes and flowed over the creature's body. As Sean watched, the spider began to transform.

The shimmering pink light faded, and a tall woman stood in its place. She had long, brown hair and pale white skin. The most startling thing about her were her large eyes, which were a bright shade of pink. She wore a long, flowing gown that matched their color exactly.

"I am the Sorceress," she said.

Go to page 85.

Continued from page 39

As the walls closed in, Sean struggled to decide what to do. In most of the fantasy books he had read, there were always puzzles and challenges for the main character to find out. The Cave of Transformation must be some kind of puzzle. Now he just had to solve it—fast.

The clue had to be in the words engraved on the door. "Step lightly but wisely," Sean repeated aloud. He studied the pictures on the stones.

"Sean, we must do something!" Taran yelled. The sharp spikes were only inches away . . .

Then Sean noticed the engraved picture of the owl. *Lightly but wisely.* Owls were supposed to be wise, weren't they?

"Let's step on the owl," Sean said.

Taran didn't hesitate. He sprang onto the owl stone, and Sean jumped right behind him.

The walls stopped moving. There was a groaning sound as a stone doorway slid open in front of them.

"We did it," Sean breathed.

"I hope so," said Taran. "Who knows what we will find inside? Maybe another trap."

Sean gripped the book tightly. Whatever waited for them, he had a feeling the book would help them get through it.

The boys carefully inched their way toward the open door, trying to avoid being scratched by the sharp spikes. Sean couldn't make out anything inside the door except a hollow darkness. He knew that he could find just about anything once he'd crossed through the doorway. After all—he had somehow been transported inside a book, hadn't he? Anything was possible!

The boys stepped through the doorway together, then stopped, hesitant to move ahead. Sean was relieved, at least, that Taran seemed as nervous as he felt.

Then they both noticed the glow.

A faint yellow gleam sprang up a few feet ahead of them. Could this be the magical stone they'd been looking for? Step by step they moved toward it.

As they got closer, Sean saw that a yellow stone about the size of a baseball gleamed on a pillar. He and Taran gathered around the stone.

"This must be it," Sean whispered. It felt like he'd uncovered buried treasure—or better.

"What do we do?" Taran asked.

Sean had no idea. But before Sean could answer, he felt the book stir in his hands. The cover opened, and the pages began to flip on their own.

Then the pages stopped. The book was open

to two blank pages.

Sean stared in wonder as the stone seemed to grow brighter. A yellow light glowed on the pages, and in the light Sean could see words appearing.

"What does it say?" Taran asked.

Sean read aloud.

"As the gem grows, so does its power. The power to turn trolls to stone. The power to grow life where none exists. The power to travel through time and dimension. But the stone may only be used once, for then its powers are no more.

Taran was practically jumping up and down with excitement. "The power to turn trolls to stone!" he cried. "It is just what we need. Sean, you have saved us!"

"Uh, sure," Sean replied. His mind was racing. Turning trolls to stone was one thing—but the power to travel through dimensions? That meant the stone could help him get home.

But the book said the stone could be used only once. If he used the stone to get home, then Taran's people would have no way to fight the trolls. But if he used the stone to help Taran's people, Sean might be stuck in Liasa forever. Sean had no idea what the right decision was.

"Let us hurry, Sean," Taran said. "We can use the stone to stop the trolls before they attack the village."

If Sean uses the stone to help Taran's people fight the trolls, go to page 96.

If Sean uses the stone to try to get home, go to page 132.

Continued from page 26

Sean studied the tiles. If there was a pattern, he didn't see one. The note had said to choose carefully, but Sean had no idea which one was right.

"I might as well pick one," he reasoned. "Otherwise, I'll be stuck here."

Sean used the eenie-meenic-minie-mo method and picked the tile engraved with the picture of the candle. He put the tile in the empty place on the wall. Grooves in the stone held it in place.

Then he stepped back.

Whoosh!

An intense heat filled the chamber. Before Sean could react, a huge circle of fire sprung up from the cave floor, surrounding him. The flames leaped higher than Sean's head, almost touching the ceiling.

Panic began to set in as Sean turned around the circle, looking for a way out. There wasn't one.

"I guess I shouldn't have picked the candle!" Sean said.

THE END

Continued from page 139

Sean decided to try pointing at the rat. Why else would there be a rat on the handle of the sword?

Sean pointed his left finger at the rat handle.

Nothing happened.

"Uh, abracadabra?" he tried.

The Baka troll's club came down, knocking the sword out of Sean's hand. The blow knocked Sean to the ground.

The huge troll towered over him, raising his club to strike again.

"Help!" Sean yelled.

Whap!

A stone flew through the air, hitting the troll square in the forehead. He staggered, then fell backward.

Sean looked up to see Joki in a nearby tree. Joki nodded, and Sean waved at him gratefully. It was the second time Joki had saved his life in twenty-four hours.

The Baka troll had fallen on the magic sword, and Sean had no way to move the troll aside and try again. He had no weapon, no way to fight. He climbed up into the tree with Joki.

"Thanks," Sean said. "What can I do?"

"Keep handing me stones," Joki said. "I can

shoot more that way."

Sean grabbed Joki's bag and handed the little troll stone after stone. Joki was a good shot. Every time he hit a Baka in the forehead, it fell to the ground.

"That's their weak spot," Joki explained.

Most of the trolls were experts with their slingshots. But for every Baka they took down, three more Bakas stomped down through the woods. There were just too many for the trolls to fight off.

The sound of the horn rang through the village again. Sean heard Xalor's voice rise over the battle. "Retreat!"

Joki looked crestfallen. "I know she is right," he said. "But how I hate to leave our home!"

Sean followed Joki down the tree. The trolls were beginning to flee the village, carrying their belongings in sacks and carts. Xalor walked through the crowds.

"Take heart, people," she said. "Raza the Rat Star will lead us. Like the mighty rat, we too will survive."

"Raza the rat?" Sean asked Joki.

"Our legends say that the star is the eye of Raza, the great rat," Joki explained.

Sean groaned inwardly. That explained the rat on the handle of the sword.

"Hurry, Sean," Joki said. "We must flee!"

Sean ran alongside Joki. He had no idea where they were going—or if he would ever get home.

"I should have pointed the sword at the star," Sean moaned.

THE END

Continued from page 76

"H-h-hello," Sean breathed. He had never met anyone who looked so beautiful and so strange at the same time.

"You have passed my challenges," the Sorceress said. Her voice sounded musical, with layers of sound behind it. "Well done."

"Thanks," Sean said. He wasn't sure what he was supposed to say or do.

"You may ask me for a favor," said the Sorceress. "If I am able, I will grant it."

"I'd like to go back to my home," Sean said. "I kind of got here by mistake."

The Sorceress nodded. "I can do that," she said. She waved her left hand.

Out of thin air, four doors appeared in the garden. They weren't attached to anything, and they seemed to hover a few inches off the ground.

The Sorceress opened her right hand, and Sean saw a key in her palm. She came toward Sean, and it looked as though she was floating. Then she handed him the key.

"One of the doors will take you home," she said. "You may try the key once and only once."

Sean took the key from her and resisted the urge to complain. He had been through so many challenges already and had passed each one. And now he had to do one more! It wasn't fair.

Still, Sean didn't want to anger the Sorceress. He had seen how powerful her magic could be.

"Thank you," Sean said. He walked up to the doors. How was he supposed to know which door to go through?

As Sean got closer, he saw that each door was different. There was a small, round window on the front of each door, slightly higher than Sean's head. He walked up to one of the doors and stood on his toes.

On the first door, he saw what looked like the garden of the Sorceress, filled with growing plants and trees. It looked real, almost like he was spying on the scene through a window.

He walked to the second door. Through the window, he saw leaves blowing in the breeze. They danced and dipped in the wind.

At the third door, Sean saw a volcano through the window. Hot lava erupted from its crown.

Sean walked to the last door. Through the window, he saw a flowing river.

The images had to be some kind of a clue, Sean knew. But which one would get him home?

He looked down at the key. It was heavy and made of sturdy silver. Images of flying birds were engraved along its length.

Sean looked at the birds, then at the doors.

He had to use the key in one of the doors. But which one?

If Sean chooses the first door, go to page 142.

If Sean chooses the second door, go to page 40.

If Sean chooses the third door, go to page 100.

If Sean chooses the fourth door, go to page 92.

"We cannot defeat the trolls by ourselves," Taran said. "Malchior will be fair. I promise."

Taran seemed so certain. "All right," Sean said. He hoped his new friend was right.

The boys crept out of the chambers, and Sean followed Taran to a small hut on the edge of the village. Strange symbols were carved into the wooden door.

"This is Malchior's home," Taran said.

"One second," Sean said. He quickly looked around. If Taran was wrong, Sean might need the book to get home. He ran to a nearby rock and tucked the book underneath. Then he hurried back to Malchior's door.

"Let's knock," Sean said.

But before they could, the door opened. Malchior stood there, a stern look on his face.

"You boys have disobeyed us." It was a statement, not a question.

"Please, Malchior," Taran said. "You must listen. Sean can read the book. It tells of a way to stop the trolls. Sean can help us."

Malchior scowled. "You dare question the elders?"

The old man went into his cabin and came out carrying a large horn. He blew on the horn, and soon the whole village had gathered around.

"Taran and the newcomer have disobeyed the elders," Malchior cried. "The punishment is banishment!"

Taran looked like he was going to cry. Sean felt bad for him. He didn't care if he never saw the village again. But this was Taran's home.

"Don't blame Taran," Sean said. "I forced him to come with me. He tried to stop me. Banish me but not him."

A cry went up from the villagers. The elders huddled together and whispered. Finally, Malchior spoke. "Taran may stay," he said. "But the newcomer must leave immediately."

Sean thought quickly. "Can I take some stuff with me, like water or food?" he asked. "You guys don't want me to die out there."

Malchior nodded, and Sean gave Taran a glance.

"I'll do it," Taran said, understanding. He ran off and returned a few minutes later with a cloth sack. Sean covertly felt the sack. Just as he had hoped, Taran had put the book inside.

"Thank you for trying to help us," Taran said. "I hope you find a way home."

Sean nodded. "Good luck with the trolls."

The villagers walked Sean to the edge of the village, back to the trail in the woods that he and

Taran had first traveled. The woods looked sinister and spooky in the dark. He took a deep breath and forged ahead.

Sean tried to come up with a plan as he walked. The book had to contain a way for him to get back home—it had to. When he felt he had gone a safe distance from the village, he leaned back against a tree and opened the book. A shaft of moonlight lit up the pages.

Sean looked through the book until sunrise. Finally, he came across something that might help him.

"A magic portal," Sean read. "Capable of transporting the traveler to other times and dimensions. That's got to be it!"

A map showed the location of the portal, which seemed to be some kind of cave. Sean frowned. The portal was located on the other side of the troll village. He'd have to cross through the village to get there.

There had to be some other way. Sean studied the map. He could go around the troll village, through something called the Plains of Despair. A picture of a skull was drawn over the plains. It didn't look too friendly.

Sean wasn't sure what to do. He knew the trolls weren't friendly. But if he could sneak past the trolls, he wouldn't have to go far. Should he take his chances with the trolls—or try the Plains of Despair?

If Sean decides to travel through the troll village, go to page 114.

If Sean decides to travel through the Plains of Despair, go to page 126.

Continued from page 87

Sean looked at the fourth door, and then at the key. The birds on the key reminded him of birds he had seen on the river. It might be the fourth door.

Sean took a deep breath. He had to try. He put the key in the door and turned it.

The door swung open, and Sean suddenly found himself next to a flowing riverbank. The sky above was blue, not pink. He realized he was back at the exact spot where he had first entered Liasa! Then that would mean . . .

He turned to his right to see the two-headed exo beast charging toward him once again.

Sean didn't hesitate. He plunged into the river. "I hope this time I get things right!" he said.

THE END

Continued from page 55

Sean reached down and grabbed the helix cube.

I must be crazy, he thought. But something deep inside him pushed him on. He wanted to at least try to help the trolls—even though he probably wouldn't succeed.

Sean ran back to the heart of the cave. It was empty. He thanked his luck and started to pry open the lid of the box.

But before he could open it, a thunderous sound filled the chamber. Baka trolls poured in from every passageway, surrounding Sean. He felt like a mouse in a room full of elephants.

"HUMAN!" the Baka trolls all cried.

Sean struggled with the latch. He had no idea what would happen when the box opened. For all he knew, he would be wiped out along with the trolls. There was no way for him to run.

But it was his only chance.

The Baka trolls charged on Sean, swinging heavy wooden clubs. Sean ducked, furiously pulling on the latch.

The box opened.

Immediately, a blinding white light shot out from the cube, filling every corner of the chamber. Sean dropped the box and shaded his eyes.

The trolls howled as the light rays hit them.

Sean watched in amazement as they evaporated into thin air one by one.

The light rays shot out of the chamber into the passageways, and a chorus of angry howls flowed through the cave. Sean put his hands over his ears to block out the sound.

A few minutes later, the cries died down. The light faded and finally disappeared, and the lid to the helix cube snapped shut.

Sean picked up the box and stared at it for a moment. It had worked! He couldn't believe it. He sprinted out of the chamber, through the cave, and down the hill. He had to tell Joki!

The troll was waiting for him at the bottom of the hill. His round face bore a big grin.

"I saw the light!" he said. "You did it, Sean! You did it!"

Sean was exhausted, but the pride and excitement of what he had done kept him moving back through the trail. He couldn't wait to see the looks on the faces of the trolls when he told them the good news.

It was the middle of the night by the time they reached the village, but the trolls were waiting for them. Bonfires had been lit throughout the enclave. A cry went up when Sean and Joki emerged from the woods. Xalor walked to the front of the crowd to receive the news.

"He has done it," Joki said. "The Baka trolls are no more!"

A cheer went up from the villagers. Before he knew what was happening, Sean found himself being carried on the shoulders of a small group of trolls and led throughout the village.

Sean basked in the glory for a while. But something was tugging at him—the Portal of Time and Dimension. His adventure in Liasa had been amazing, but he missed his home and his family.

"I should try to get home soon," Sean called to Xalor. "I think I know how to get there."

Xalor nodded. "We will help you get home in the morning, Sean. First, you must feast—and rest."

Go to page 122.

Continued from page 80

Taran sounded so hopeful. Using the stone to get home would help him, but using it to destroy the trolls would help many more people. He had to help them and hope for the best—that he could get home some other way.

"Let's go," Sean said. The boys left the chamber and stood at the entrance to the first chamber. Before they could step on the tiles, each one flipped over, revealing a flat, blank surface.

"I guess it's safe to cross," Sean guessed.

The boys walked across the chamber and faced the stone door. Sean tried knocking three times. Just as before, the door slid open.

Taran began to walk quickly.

"If we hurry, we can reach the troll village by daybreak, before they attack," he said.

"Right," said Sean. "Sounds like a plan."

The boys walked back toward Taran's village, being careful to stay on the outside, out of sight of the villagers. Then they got on the path through the woods back to the troll village.

"How will we use the stone once we get there?" Taran asked nervously. Sean realized that heading back to the trolls couldn't be easy for Taran, who had come so close to being troll food.

"The answer must be somewhere in the book,"

Sean replied. "We'll check it out before we get too close."

Taran nodded, and the boys kept walking. The first rays of morning sunlight were peeking through the darkness as they neared the troll village.

Sean stopped. The woods were beginning to thin; soon they'd have no cover. He leaned against a tree and opened the book on his lap.

"All right," he said. "How do I use the stone to stop the trolls?"

The gem began to glow in his hand, and the pages of the book flipped back and forth. Then they stopped. Sean read from the page:

"To use the stone against trolls, hold it upright in your right hand," the wizard said. "Turn three times to the right. Then throw the stone forcefully into the earth. The stone will explode, causing every troll within a field's length to turn to stone forever."

"All of the trolls turned to stone . . ." Taran said, his eyes shining. "Wouldn't that be wonderful?"

"We should probably get them all out in the open," Sean suggested. "To make sure it works."

A determined look crossed Taran's face. "I know what to do," he said. "Leave it to me."

Without another word, Taran ran toward the

troll village.

"Taran, no!" Sean cried.

"Come and get it! Come and get your breakfast!" Taran yelled.

Sean ran after his friend, then stopped. One by one, huge trolls came lumbering out of the nearby caves. Each one was as huge and ugly as the next. They each carried large, spiked clubs. At the sight of Taran, they charged forward, growling and hooting.

Sean held up the stone in his right hand. He'd have to act fast. He turned in a circle— once, twice, three times. Then he threw the stone like a baseball.

Blam! The stone exploded, filling the sky with a shower of yellow fireworks. Sean covered his head with his arms and ducked.

When the noise died down, Sean stood up again. Taran stood in the middle of the trolls, a huge grin on his face.

Each troll looked like a big, stone statue!

"We did it!" Taran cried. "Thank you, thank you, Sean. You have saved my people."

"You're welcome," Sean said. It felt good to help Taran. But the thought that he might never see his family again suddenly hit him. It was hard to be happy.

The boys returned to Taran's village and told

their story. At first no one believed them, but Malchior agreed to return with them to the troll village. At the sight of the stone trolls, he smiled and nodded.

"Well done," he said. He turned to Sean. "Our village owes you a great debt."

"Maybe you can give me a place to live," Sean said glumly. "That stone was my only way home. I'll never get back now."

Malchior stroked his beard. "Show me where you threw the stone."

Sean took him to the spot, and Malchior began to search the ground. Finally, he stood up. He held what looked like a small, yellow seed.

"I knew about the stone but did not know how to find it," Malchior said. "It is true that the stone can only be used once. But the stone will grow again. In one year, it will be powerful enough to send you home. You may live with us until then."

Sean stared at the seed. One year. That wasn't too long to wait.

"Thanks," Sean said.

THE END

Continued from page 87

Sean wasn't sure which door to pick. The key
didn't seem to go with any of the doors.

He closed his eyes and waved his finger around.
Then he opened his eyes to see that he was pointing
at the third door.

Sean walked to the door, put the key in the lock,
and turned it. The door swung open.

A huge creature stood behind the door. It was
nearly three times as tall as Sean, with green skin;
long, sharp fingernails; and a hideous face. The
creature wore animal skins and carried a big wooden
club studded with spikes.

Sean stepped back.

"That is a Baka troll," said the Sorceress behind
him. "You have picked the wrong door. But I will
give you one more chance. If you fight the Baka
and defeat him, I will send you home."

Sean didn't answer right away. How was he
supposed to beat this monster?

Then Sean thought of his mom and his dad and
his brothers. He missed them a lot. If getting home
meant fighting the troll, he would do it.

"Okay," Sean said.

The Sorceress smiled. She waved her left
hand, and a small sword appeared in Sean's
right hand. She nodded at the Baka troll, and he

stepped into the garden.

Sean began waving his sword around like crazy, trying desperately to stab at the troll. The troll watched, amused. Then it lifted up a huge foot and kicked Sean to the ground.

"Too easy," growled the troll. It stepped on Sean's chest, pinning him to the ground. He couldn't get away. The Baka lifted his club, ready to strike Sean . . .

And then the Baka disappeared. Sean scrambled to his feet, relieved and confused. The Sorceress appeared in front of him.

"I admire your bravery," she said. "You must want to get home very much."

Sean nodded.

The Sorceress handed him the key again. "Try the second door."

Sean walked up to the second door. "Thanks," he told the Sorceress. Then he turned the key.

He stepped into his kitchen. His mom was cutting up a banana for Henry. Jake was eating cereal.

"My, you slept late," said Mrs. Flatbush. "Were you up reading again?"

"Of course he was," said Jake. "He's a Worm."

Sean smiled. He didn't even feel mad at Jake. He was home.

THE END

Continued from page 110

The air inside the portal tingled with electricity. Sean remembered Xalor's instructions. He closed his eyes and concentrated.

"Home. Back in my bedroom in Bleaktown. Last night," he said out loud.

Sean opened his eyes. To his amazement, he found himself back in his room! Moonlight streamed through the window.

The door to his bedroom opened, and his mother poked her head inside the room.

"Sean, are you up late reading again?" she asked sleepily.

"Uh, I was just getting up to use the bathroom," he lied.

Mrs. Flatbush frowned. "Please get some sleep, Sean. It's late."

"Okay," Sean said. Then he thought of something. "Mom, what day is it?"

Mrs. Flatbush shook her head. "Well, a minute ago it was Friday. But it's one minute after midnight. So I guess it's officially Saturday—and way past your bedtime!"

"Sorry, Mom," Sean said. He couldn't believe it. The portal had worked perfectly! It was like he hadn't been away for any time at all.

Sean's mom closed the door and Sean sank

onto his bed, exhausted. His pajamas were filthy, so he peeled them off and put on some new ones. As he sat down again, he spotted *War of the Trolls* lying open on his bed.

Sean quickly closed the cover. He wasn't going to make the mistake of reading it after midnight again. He had had enough adventures for now. In fact, he should probably take the book back to the junk shop. It wasn't safe to have around.

Sean put the book on the floor and put his head on his pillow. He'd take the book back tomorrow . . .

. . . or maybe not. He missed Joki and the trolls already. Why couldn't he go back and visit? He could always get back using the portal.

Of course, things might not work out so great next time. But still, it might be worth a try.

Sean fell asleep, dreaming of trolls and a magic sword.

THE END

Continued from page 26

Choose carefully, the note said. Sean studied the puzzle.

Tree. Feather. Flame. Drop of Water. Mountain. Butterfly. Candle.

There had to be some kind of pattern, some kind of connection. He took his time, and after a few minutes noticed something.

The flame and the candle both had to do with fire, and they were both third in the pattern. Maybe the other words were related, too.

He looked at the feather and butterfly. They both had to do with animals that flew.

Then he got it. The puzzle was about the four elements! The flame and candle represented fire. The feather and butterfly represented air. The tree and mountain were both things associated with the earth. And the drop of water represented water, of course. It was almost too easy.

He looked at the tiles on the table. Mountain. Cloud. Candle. Icicle. It had to be the icicle—frozen water!

With a shaking hand, Sean placed the icicle tile in the empty spot on the wall. A groove in the stone held the tile in place. Then he stepped back.

The wall began to slide to the side. It wasn't a

wall at all—it was a door! Beyond the door, Sean saw a strange land covered by a pale pink sky. A blast of cold air swept into the chamber.

This must be the way to the Sorceress, he realized. He stepped through the chamber and shivered. He was on the shore of a frozen pond. A light coating of crunchy snow covered the ground, freezing his bare feet. He looked for a path but didn't find one.

Then a white piece of paper fluttered down from the sky. Sean caught it. It was another note, written in the same pink ink.

Free the frozen fish to move on.
All it takes is one word.
The word can be found in a friend.
Say the word, free the fish, and continue.
Say the wrong word, and your journey is over.

Sean wasn't sure what the riddle meant, at first. He studied it. A word found in a friend . . .

Sean had two ideas of what the word might be. It could be "fire." Or it could be "nice." He had a different reason for choosing each one.

He hesitated. He had to make sure to pick the right word—or his journey would be over!

If Sean says the word "fire," go to page 129.
If Sean says the word "nice," go to page 140.

Continued from page 139

"Please work!" Sean whispered. Just as the Baka's club came down, Sean raised the sword, pointing right at the Raza star in the sky.

Instantly, a ray of light streamed from the star, illuminating the sword. The metal suddenly felt hot in Sean's hand, but he held on.

After it hit the sword, the light splintered in all directions, sending lightning bolts shooting out all over the village. Sean gasped. Had he done something wrong?

But the bolts didn't hurt any villagers. Instead, miraculously, each lightning bolt hit a Baka troll right in the forehead. As each Baka was hit, it instantly vaporized.

The shooting bolts lit up the village, and Sean thought it looked more amazing than any fire-works show he had ever seen. He kept the sword raised in the air until the last lightning bolt shot out. Then the sword went dim.

Sean quickly dropped the sword, waving his hands to try to cool them off. They felt like they were on fire.

There was a hush in the troll village as the trolls realized what had happened. Then, as one, they let out a great cheer.

Joki ran up to Sean, breathless.

"I saw the whole thing from my tree," he said. "You did it, Sean! You have saved our village!"

Before Sean knew what was happening, he found himself being lifted up by a multitude of troll arms. They carried Sean through the village, chanting his name.

The procession stopped in the village center, where the trolls set Sean back down on the ground. Xalor approached him.

"The old wizard who left us this sword must have known we would need it someday," she said. "Thank you, Sean. Our people owe you a great debt."

Sean shook his head. "Joki saved me from that beast thing back at the river. You guys don't owe me anything."

Xalor smiled. "Still, if there is anything we can do for you . . . I know you are far from your home."

Sean suddenly felt sad. His whole adventure in Liasa had been amazing—almost unreal. But the thought of never seeing his family again was too hard to take.

"Do you think there's a way I could get back?" he asked. "Joki said something about a Sorceress."

Xalor frowned. "That path is dangerous. Perhaps there is something in the book. Come."

Sean followed Xalor through the crowd to her

hut, where she produced *War of the Trolls*.

"The book holds many secrets," she said. "Perhaps it holds a secret that can help you."

Xalor looked through the book, and Sean looked over her shoulder. They must have searched for about an hour when Xalor stopped.

"Ah," she said, pointing. Sean read the text.

In the cave of the Baka trolls is a Portal of Time and Dimension. The Bakas are too primitive to understand its purpose. But the secret of the portal is easy. Step inside, and concentrate on where and when you want to go. The portal will take you there.

"There should be no more Bakas in the caves," Xalor said. "Can you wait until morning? I will send Joki with you."

Sean nodded. "No problem," he said. He wouldn't mind staying in Liasa just a little longer.

Sean stayed awake through the rest of the night, feasting and dancing with the trolls. When the sun rose, he and Joki set back out for the Baka caves.

This time, they didn't stop at the edge of the woods. They both walked toward the cave entrance, following the path into the cave. They didn't go far before they found an archway in the wall. Over the arch were inscribed the words:

"The Portal of Time and Dimension."

"Well, that was easy," Sean said. He turned to Joki. "Thanks again for saving me."

Joki bowed his head. "Our people owe you our lives, as well, Sean. We will sing songs about you to our children for years to come."

Sean felt really proud. He shook Joki's hand. "I'll never forget you," he said.

"Nor will I," Joki replied.

Sean broke away from Joki and stepped through the archway.

Go to page 102.

Sean was impatient. "Let's try the start of night," he said. "That's coming soon."

"It is risky," Xalor said. "You may live here with us as long as you like."

"Thanks," Sean said. "I really like your village. But I miss my family."

Xalor nodded. "I understand," she said. "We will miss you, Sean."

Before Sean knew it, the sun was low in the sky. Xalor approached him and handed him the helix cube.

"It is time," she said.

The whole troll village followed Sean as Xalor led him to the crossroads in the center of the village, where two main paths met.

"What do I do?" Sean asked.

"Just open the lid," Xalor said. "The helix cube will take you where you want to go."

Sean nodded. "Thanks," he said. He turned to Joki. "Thanks again for saving me."

"You will always have a brother in Liasa," Joki said.

Sean felt sad about leaving. But he knew he couldn't stay. He opened the silver clasp on the helix cube and lifted the lid.

A white light shot out of the cube, blinding

him. Every cell in Sean's body tingled with an electric pulse.

Then the light dimmed, and Sean saw that he was back in his own room! Moonlight streamed through the window.

"I made it," he whispered. But how long had he been gone? He checked the date and time on his computer. It was one minute after midnight—exactly one minute after he had been sucked into the book.

So no time has passed here, Sean realized. His family didn't even know he had been gone. Sean sank into his bed and fell into a deep sleep.

The next morning, Sean woke up and looked at *War of the Trolls,* which lay open on his covers. He picked it up and began to read. He missed Joki and the trolls already.

What he found on the pages startled him.

Joki aimed his slingshot at the exo beast. The beast fell, and the human boy climbed down from the tree.

"I'm Sean," the boy said. "Thank you for saving me."

Sean gasped. That was him. His story! He would always be a part of the book now.

"Sean, time for breakfast!" his mother called.

"One minute, Mom," Sean called back.

He had a lot of reading to do.

THE END

Continued from page 131

Sean wasn't sure what to do. He looked at the apple tree. The red apples looked the biggest and the juiciest. Maybe they were what the fish wanted.

Sean walked to the tree and picked a red apple. He carried it back to the fish.

"Are you sure?" the fish asked.

Sean wasn't sure. But he had to try something. He nodded, and reached down and placed the apple in the fish's mouth. The fish swallowed it in one gulp. Then the fish frowned.

"Oh, dear," the fish said. "That can't be right."

The fish belched, and in the next instant, Sean found himself in another landscape. The sky overhead was deep red. He stood on top of a hill. Below him stretched out a maze made up of stone walls.

A Fire Apple will get you lost.

Fire Apple. Red was the color of fire. He had picked the Fire Apple, and now he was lost in the maze.

Sean trudged down the hill. He might as well start. There was always a way to get out of a maze, right? It might take a long time, but he'd have to try.

He had no other choice.

THE END

Continued from page 91

Sean decided to check out the troll village. If it looked too dangerous, he could always try the other way. He ate some of the food and water that Taran had packed for him and then started off down the trail.

He knew he was near the troll village when the woods began to thin out and a stale smell filled the air. The land of the trolls was bare and lifeless, as though nothing good could grow there. He shuddered, remembering the huge troll that had chased them.

As he got closer to the village, Sean heard the dense tattoo of a drum. Sean's heart beat quickly. The trolls were awake—and up to something.

Sean got as close as he dared and then hid behind a bare, thin tree. He cautiously peered into the village.

He gasped. What looked like a hundred trolls were gathered in a circle. One troll sat in the center, beating on a large, standing drum. The other trolls faced him, pounding huge wooden clubs into the ground.

They must be preparing for battle, Sean realized. *They're going to attack Taran's village.*

Sean shook his head. He could have helped them. But it wasn't his problem anymore. He had to find that magic portal and get back home.

Sean surveyed the situation. The trolls seemed preoccupied with their war chant or whatever it was they were doing. They wouldn't see him if he snuck by. And they wouldn't hear him, either, with all the racket they were making.

He decided it was worth the risk. Taking a deep breath, Sean cautiously stepped out from behind the tree. He bent over, keeping low to the ground. Then he quickly made it to the next scraggly tree he could find.

So far, so good. Sean just had to get past the circle of trolls, and he'd have a clear path to the portal. He set off again.

Sean hadn't gone far when suddenly, the sound of the drum and clubs stopped. The trolls were sniffing the air with their cavernous nostrils.

"I smell human," one of the trolls growled.

"HUMAN!" the trolls yelled as one.

Sean froze as every single troll turned at once and stared at him.

Then they charged.

Sean ran. He didn't even dare to look back. He just willed his legs to go as fast as they could.

Luckily for Sean, the trolls were fairly clumsy, and many of them tripped over one another as they scrambled to get to him. Sean had a decent lead.

Then he tripped over a rock.

Wham! Sean got the wind knocked out of him as he landed face-first in the dirt. The sack flew out of his hands, and the book flew out of the sack, landing open a few inches from his face.

Sean regained his breath and tried to get to his feet, but he was too late. The trolls surrounded him.

"HUMAN! HUMAN! HUMAN!" they chanted. Each one had sharp claws the size of one of Sean's arms and a gaping mouth filled with pointy teeth.

Sean had never been so afraid in his whole life. His head felt light, like he might faint.

Then he noticed the book. The pages were flipping by themselves. Then they suddenly stopped. Sean glanced at the words on the page.

A Spell for Speed

To achieve a speed faster than a shooting star, say these words three times: Rapidare, celeritous, prontado.

"HUMAN! HUMAN! HUMAN!" the trolls chanted. They came in closer.

Sean struggled to find his breath. He picked up the book. *"Rapidare, celeritous, prontado. Rapidare, celeritous, prontado. Rapidare, celeritous, prontado."*

Before he realized what was happening, Sean's feet took off. He tore through the dirt, sending him scurrying between the legs of a giant troll like a whirlwind. Less than a second later, he found himself on the outskirts of the troll village. The trolls were so far away, he could barely make out their outlines on the horizon.

Sean's feet abruptly stopped. He looked at the book.

"Thanks," he said. Then he looked through the book until he found the map that led to the magic portal.

He realized he wasn't far at all. In a few minutes, he found himself at the mouth of a cave. A stone above the cave was engraved with instructions:

ENTER THE PORTAL WITHIN
SPEAK THY DESTINATION
FOLLOW THY PATH

"I hope this works," Sean said. He stepped inside the cave. There was nothing magical-looking about it at all. But he might as well try.

"Bleaktown, my bedroom, last night," Sean said out loud.

There was a rumbling sound, and a hole in the

cave opened up. Purple light swirled within.

Follow Thy Path, the instructions had said. Sean stepped inside the tunnel. The swirling light engulfed him. He took two steps. When his foot landed on the third step, he found himself back in his bedroom. He wasn't holding the book anymore. It lay on his bed, open to the page that had sent him to Liasa in the first place.

"Wow," Sean said. It had worked!

Sean closed the book and picked it up. *War of the Trolls* was no ordinary book. He wanted to know more about it. And he knew one man who could tell him.

The strange little man who owned the junk shop.

Go to page 143.

Continued from page 131

Sean went over the song in his head. Fire Apple. Grass Apple. Sun Apple.

He smiled. It was almost too easy.

The Fire Apple had to be red. The Grass Apple had to be green. And the Sun Apple had to be yellow. *A Sun Apple will lead the way.*

The yellow apple was the right one. He knew it. He walked to the tree and plucked a yellow apple. Then he walked back to the fish.

"Are you sure?" the fish asked.

"Yes," Sean said confidently.

"Then go ahead and feed me," the fish said. It opened its mouth wide.

Sean knelt down and popped the yellow apple into the fish's mouth. The fish swallowed the apple in one gulp. Then it nodded its head.

"Hits the spot," the fish said.

Then the fish began to grow.

Sean stepped back as the fish transformed before his eyes. It grew to the size of a small elephant. A long neck stretched out from its body, and its head became more sculpted and dragon-like. Its tail curved up gracefully out of the water.

"Cool," Sean said.

"How interesting," the fish said. "I believe I have transformed into a sea serpent."

That worried Sean for a second. "Did I do something wrong?"

"Oh, no," said the fish. "I could use a change. And now I can take you to your next challenge."

Sean groaned inwardly. Another challenge! Would he ever get to see the Sorceress?

"Climb on my back," the fish—or sea serpent— said.

Sean grabbed onto the sea serpent's back, expecting it to be slimy. But it was firm, and he got a good enough grip to climb on top.

"Hang on," the sea serpent said. The creature turned around in the water and began to glide across the pond.

The pale pink sky and pink water made the whole landscape look like another planet, Sean thought as they made their way across the pond. It had to be some kind of magical land—the home of the Sorceress, he hoped.

They reached the other side of the pond in just a few minutes. Sean saw a round stone wall on the land offshore.

"Better climb down," said the sea serpent. "It's time for your next challenge."

Sean did as he was told and landed on the grassy bank of the pond. "What do I do?"

"You've got to get behind the wall, of course," said the sea serpent. "But you will see. Good luck. You've been much more interesting than I expected."

The sea serpent's praise gave Sean a boost of confidence. He waved good-bye and walked up to the stone wall. He found himself facing a thick wooden door locked with a large metal padlock. Hanging on the stone wall were two keys. And tacked to the door was another note:

Only one key opens the door.
This key has something in common with the sun in the sky, an owl's eye, and a currant pie.
Choose carefully, and your journey will soon be at an end.

Sean studied the keys. The prongs on the bottom of both keys looked the same. But one was silver with a circle on top. The other was gold with a diamond shape on top.

Sean was almost there now. He had to pick the right key.

If Sean chooses the silver key with the circle-shaped top, go to page 61.

If Sean chooses the gold key with the diamond-shaped top, go to page 52.

Continued from page 95

Sean and the trolls celebrated for hours, eating and dancing as a circle of trolls beat drums and shook rattles. Sean fell asleep in Joki's cabin on a soft mat. When he woke up, sun streamed through the window. Joki was already awake.

"Time to go, Sean," he said. "I will miss you. We all will miss you."

Joki, Xalor, and a small party of trolls accompanied Sean back to the cave of the Baka trolls. The dim passageways were quiet and empty. When they came to the Portal of Time and Dimension, Xalor turned to Sean.

"The Baka trolls were too stupid to know how to use the portal," she said. "It belonged to our people eons ago, before the Baka trolls invaded. But it is simple. When you enter, close your eyes and think about exactly when and where you want to go. When you open your eyes, you should be there."

"Thanks," Sean said. He said good-bye to all the trolls. Then he stepped into the dark portal.

The air in the portal felt different than in the rest of the cave. It made his skin tingle, as though it was somehow electrified. Sean closed his eyes and concentrated.

"Home," he whispered, imagining himself in his bedroom just as he had been the other night.

Sean didn't feel any different, but he opened his eyes, anyway. To his amazement, he found himself back in his bedroom. It was dark.

"I made it!" Sean cried. But how long had he been gone?

Sean quickly went to his computer and turned it on. The date and time flashed on the screen.

It was the same date and time that he had first entered the book. Time hadn't passed in this dimension at all!

Relieved, Sean sat down on the bed and looked for the book. He couldn't wait to read more. Maybe he could find a way to go in and out of the book whenever he wanted.

Sean turned over every blanket and piece of stray clothing. He looked in every drawer and under every piece of furniture. But he couldn't find the book anywhere.

He sat back down on the bed, disappointed. He didn't even know how the rest of the story went! The illuminated computer screen stared back at him.

Then Sean had an idea. He might not be able to read the story, but he had just been in an exciting story all his own. Maybe he could write about it.

Sean sat down at his computer and began to type . . .

War of the Trolls . . .

THE END

Continued from page 131

Sean didn't know what to do. The song didn't seem to make sense. He looked at the fish, then looked at the apple tree.

The fish's eyes were the same color green as the green apples. Maybe a green apple was the answer.

Sean walked to the tree and plucked a green apple. He walked back to the fish.

"Are you sure?" the fish asked.

Sean wasn't sure, but he didn't want the fish to know that. "Yup," he answered.

"Then go ahead and feed me," the fish said. It opened its mouth wide.

Sean crossed his fingers. He knelt down and plopped the green apple into the fish's mouth.

The fish gulped down the apple. Then it frowned.

"Oh, dear," it said. "That can't be right."

The fish turned bright green. Then it let out a terrible wail. Sean stepped back, suddenly afraid.

Before his eyes, the fish began to grow and change. Four legs sprouted from its body. Its tail grew long and thin, and green spikes popped out all along it. Two huge horns grew out of the fish's head.

"I'm a monster!" the fish wailed, and the

sound shook the branches of the apple tree.

"Uh, sorry," Sean said, backing up.

The monster sniffed the air. "Something smells good," it said. "You know, I'm still hungry. Very hungry."

"Want some more apples?" Sean asked, taking another step backward.

The monster looked at Sean and grinned. Its green eyes glimmered.

"No," the monster said. "I think I would like to eat YOU!"

THE END

Continued from page 91

Sean thought about going through the troll village. It would definitely be easier. But then he remembered the troll that had chased him and Taran—the long claws, the hideous face, the sharp fangs. He shuddered. He couldn't imagine facing that monster again, never mind a *bunch* of them.

Sean decided to give the Plains of Despair a try. Maybe it was just a scary name.

He followed the map east, away from the troll river, and over a rickety bridge that led across the river that had carried him to the trolls in the first place. He stopped to eat some of the food Taran had packed for him and to drink some water. Then he carried on.

As Sean walked, the sun rose high in the sky. He carefully followed the map. After about another hour, he reached the plains.

They look more like a swamp, Sean thought. A smell like rotten eggs reached his nostrils from the dank, murky water that stretched before him. Tall, brown reeds stood like sentinels as far as he could see. The only sign of life that he could see was the big, black flies buzzing above the surface of the shallow water.

It's not so bad, Sean tried to convince himself. He took a step forward. Sticky mud squished between his toes, but the warm water only reached up to his ankles.

Sean marched on. The sun grew hotter, and sweat trickled down his back as he walked. He felt a little dizzy and nauseous.

"It's better than fighting trolls," Sean said aloud, trying to raise his spirits. In books, characters usually sang a song or whistled a tune to pass the time when they went on adventures. Sean wasn't sure what to sing, so he burst into a loud chorus of "Happy Birthday," the only song he could remember the words to.

Then he felt something slither across his ankles.

"Whoa!" Sean screamed. A shiny, black snake as thick as his arm was crawling across his feet. Sean jumped backward, terrified, and fell.

The book slipped out of the sack, and before Sean could grab it, it sank into the thick mud.

"No!" Sean cried, forgetting about the snake. He dug through the mud, but he realized the sticky goo had sucked the book into its depths. He'd never find it.

"Oh, man," Sean moaned. He marched on, not even bothering to sing this time. He had an idea of where to find the portal, but without the book, he couldn't be sure. He'd have to take his chances.

Sean tried to move faster. He wanted to reach the portal before it got dark. If he was still stuck in the Plains of Despair then, he'd be in trouble.

Sean stopped and took a drink of water—now warm from the sun—from the flask Taran had given him. Then he stepped forward.

And sank.

The sticky mud had grabbed hold of his feet like some living organism. Sean felt himself being pulled deeper and deeper into the mud. Within seconds, he had sunk up to his knees.

"Help!" Sean screamed.

A black fly buzzed around his face. Now the mud was up to his waist.

"Help!" Sean screamed again.

But no one heard him—except the fly.

THE END

Sean retraced his line of reasoning. A word found in a friend. Maybe it was a word made up of the letters in "friend." Like "end." Or "fine." Or "fire" . . .

Fire . . . That made sense. Fire melted ice.

That answer made the most sense, Sean decided. He stepped toward the lake.

"Fire!" he called out.

A blast of hot air swept over the lake. In its wake, the snow on the ground melted, and green grass sprang up from underneath. Sean watched in amazement as a small twig rose up from the ground, then immediately grew into a tree. The tree blossomed, and then green, yellow, and red apples formed, drooping from the tree's gnarled branches.

The surface of the lake changed from a sheet of ice to gently rippling pink water. Sean stepped closer. Where was the fish?

At that moment, a head of a fish popped out of the water.

"Good job," the fish said. "It's been quite cold for so long."

Sean didn't reply at first. A talking fish? He couldn't believe it.

The fish had a silver body streaked with

rainbow colors. Its bulging eyes were bright green.

"Don't you have anything to say?" the fish asked. "I haven't had anyone to talk to for such a long time."

"Uh, hi," Sean said. "I've never talked to a fish before."

"It's just like talking to a human," the fish replied. "Only much more interesting. For example, you don't seem to be very interesting at all."

Sean wasn't sure that he liked this fish very much. But he knew he needed its help. "I'm trying to find the Sorceress," he said. "I solved the second challenge and melted the ice. Do you know what I should do next?"

"Solve the third challenge, of course," the fish said.

Sean sighed. "Can you tell me where the third challenge is?"

The fish did a backflip and then splashed back out of the water. "Why, I am your third challenge, of course," it said proudly.

Maybe the challenge is to not strangle the fish, Sean thought, growing impatient. "All right," he said. "Challenge me."

"My pleasure," said the fish. "In order to proceed to the Sorceress, you must feed me. But you must feed me the correct item."

"What correct item?" Sean asked.

The fish winked. "There's a riddle, of course."
Then the fish began to sing:

"Pick an apple from the tree.
But you must choose carefully.
A Fire Apple will get you lost.
A Grass Apple carries a heavy cost.
But a Sun Apple will lead the way.
So pick an apple. Don't delay!"

Sean tried to memorize the riddle as the fish
sang it. Sean wished he had a pen and paper. Fire
Apple? Grass Apple? Sun Apple? What was the
fish singing about?

If Sean chooses the red apple, go to page 113.

If Sean chooses the yellow apple, go to page 119.

If Sean chooses the green apple, go to page 124.

"Sure," Sean answered halfheartedly. He wanted to help Taran. He really did. But the thought of never going home again was just too painful. He'd miss his mom, his dad, and his brothers.

The boys left the chamber and stood at the entrance to the first chamber. Before they could step on the tiles, each one flipped over, revealing a flat, blank surface.

The boys walked across the chamber and faced the stone door. Sean tried knocking three times. Just as before, the door slid open.

Taran began to walk quickly.

"If we hurry, we can reach the troll village by daybreak," he said. "They are stronger at night. We can use the stone against them and save my people."

Sean stopped. Taran noticed and looked back at him. "What is wrong?" Taran asked.

Sean stared at his feet. "It's just that, if we use the stone against the trolls, I won't be able to get home," he said. "I'll be stuck here . . ."

"I am sorry," Taran said sincerely. "But what else can you do?"

Sean looked at the stone in his hand. "I could use this," he said. "Like it said in the book."

Taran's eyes widened as he realized what Sean was saying. "But then we could not use the stone against the trolls."

"I know." Sean could barely look at Taran. "But the way I figure it, your elders didn't even want us to try to find the stone. They must have some other plans to defeat the trolls, right?"

Taran nodded. "You are right," he said. "The stone belongs to you. Do with it as you wish."

"Thanks," Sean said, letting out a relieved sigh. He sat down on a nearby rock. "Now I just have to figure out how it works."

Sean opened the book and rested it on his lap. He held the stone over it.

The stone began to glow, and the pages of the book flipped in response. Then the pages were still. Sean read from the opened page.

"The stone will help you return home," the wizard told the weary traveler. "Hold it in your left hand. Then turn widdershins three times. When the third turn is complete, the magic will be done."

"Widdershins?" Sean repeated. "What does that mean?"

Taran shrugged. "Wizard talk, I guess."

Sean studied the sentence. *Widdershins* must mean a direction—like turn left or turn right. He had no idea which. He'd just have to pick one and hope nothing bad happened.

"Here goes," Sean said. He stood up and handed the book to Taran.

"This book belongs to your people," he said. "Good luck with everything."

Taran nodded.

Sean held the stone up in his left hand. He took a deep breath. He decided to turn to the right. It was just a guess, but it was worth a try. Slowly, he turned around, silently counting.

One . . . Two . . . Three . . .

The stone exploded in a blaze of light just as he completed the first turn. The blast blinded Sean, and he tumbled backward, falling to the ground.

Then the light faded. Sean's vision slowly returned.

He wasn't in Liasa anymore, that he could see. Tall buildings rose up around him.

But as Sean began to see more clearly, he realized something was wrong. The buildings gleamed in multicolored metal. The sky was a strange shade of yellow.

Suddenly, a silver flying saucer swooped down from the sky, pausing in front of Sean. A mechanical voice blared from the saucer:

"SHOW YOUR PASS, INTRUDER, OR YOU WILL BE ARRESTED."

Sean's stomach sank. He had traveled to another time and dimension, all right . . . It just wasn't the right one!

THE END

Continued from page 47

Sean couldn't imagine he'd ever be good at using a slingshot.

"I think I'll try the magic sword," he told Joki.

Joki took the sword down from the wall and handed it to Sean. The sword felt light in his hands, and Sean could see that Joki was right about the metal. It wasn't powerful enough to do damage to a Baka troll. He'd have to figure out the magic.

"How is it supposed to work?" Sean asked.

Joki shrugged. "We trolls are not much for magic," he said. "The sword was given to our village by a wizard ages ago. I don't think anyone has tried to figure it out. Magic is tricky, you know. But you might try translating the words on the handle."

Sean turned over the handle. The handle itself was shaped like the head of an animal—a mouse or a rat. On the flat part, four words had been carved into the silver:

TINPO

DROWAT

HET

ARTS

Sean frowned. He recognized the letters, but the words seemed to be in some kind of strange language—except for the last one.

"I'm going to get some rocks together for my slingshot," Joki said. "I want to get in some practice. The Bakas will probably attack at daylight."

"I guess I'll try to figure out the inscription," Sean said.

"You can use my cabin," Joki said. "Good luck."

Sean made his way back to the cabin, passing trolls scurrying about, getting ready for battle. He sat on Joki's floor and studied the handle under candlelight.

Tinpo Drowat Het Arts. Could it be in some kind of language? He took Spanish in school, but the words didn't look Spanish. And the last word, *Arts,* was English. Maybe that was some kind of clue.

Arts. Did it have something to do with the magical arts? Maybe he just had to say the words out loud, like some kind of spell.

Sean stood up, and his head brushed the ceiling of Joki's hut. He held out the sword in front of him.

"Tinpo Drowat Het Arts!" he yelled.

Nothing happened.

Sean frowned. What did wizards and magicians

do in books that he had read? Sometimes magic spells had to be read three times or maybe seven times.

Sean tried again, saying the words three times. Nothing. He tried saying the words seven times, then thirteen. Still nothing.

Sean tried everything he could think of. He danced around in a circle. He said the words backward. But nothing special happened at all.

Sean was trying to figure out what else he could try when the sound of a loud horn blared through the village. He ran outside the hut to see the trolls all running in one direction: toward the edge of the woods on the village's north end.

The trolls gathered around Xalor, who stood on top of a large rock.

"The Bakas are coming!" she said. "They hope to catch us at a disadvantage by attacking at nightfall. But we have the light of the Raza star to guide us."

Xalor pointed to the sky, where a huge star glittered in the darkness.

"The Bakas are not used to resistance," she said. "That gives us the advantage. On to victory!"

The trolls let out a cheer. Then, at Xalor's command, they divided up. The slingshot-bearers climbed up the tall trees on the outskirts of the village. The swordsmen stayed on the ground.

Sean joined the other trolls with swords. He held his sword in front of him, ready for battle, but his hands were shaking.

I should have learned how to use the slingshot, he thought regretfully. *If a Baka comes near me, I won't be able to do anything!*

Sean briefly thought about taking off and running away somewhere—anywhere—but he decided against it. All the village trolls were so brave. He had already let them down by not going into the Baka cave. He couldn't let them down again.

Then a thunderous sound filled the village. Sean saw that the trees in the woods were shaking.

Then he spotted the Baka trolls—an army of them. They stomped through the woods toward the village. Every Baka he could see was carrying a large wooden club studded with sharp spikes.

As soon as the Bakas saw the villagers, they charged forward. The swordsmen ran ahead, waving their weapons.

To Sean's amazement, he saw one of the Baka go down before any of the swordsmen reached him. It seemed to be raining stones all of a sudden, and Sean realized it was the slingshot-bearers shooting from the trees.

A few more of the Bakas went down, but not all of them. The rest converged on the swordsmen, swinging their clubs.

Sean froze. He didn't want to run away. But he couldn't move forward, either. There were so many Baka trolls! Each one seemed more hideous than the next, and they carried a smell like rotting meat into the village with them.

One of the Bakas spotted Sean and began to march toward him. Sean unfroze—but he had no idea what to do. He tried saying the words again.

"Tinpo Drowat Het Arts!"

That's when it hit him. The words weren't in a strange language.

They were scrambled!

"Point toward the . . . arts?" That didn't make sense. The last word could be "star." Or was it "rats"?

The Baka raised his club, ready to strike. Sean had to think quickly. He could point the sword toward that big star in the sky. But maybe he was supposed to point at the rat on the handle. He knew he had to do *something*—fast!

If Sean points toward the star in the sky, go to page 107.

If Sean points toward the rat on the handle, go to page 82.

A word found in a friend? Sean thought. A friend was someone nice, right? The word could be "nice." That rhymed with ice. And magic stuff always rhymed, right?

Sean decided to try it. He faced the lake.

"Nice!" he called out.

A bitter cold wind swept across the lake. The wind wrapped around Sean like a blanket. It picked him up and carried him through the air and over the frozen water.

Below him, the ice cracked, revealing an opening in the water. The wind let go of Sean, and he fell into the crack.

He braced for the shock as the cold water hit him. He tried to swim to the top of the lake, but the ice sealed shut above him before he could get near.

Sean shivered. Then he heard a voice next to him.

"Nice to meet you." It was the fish! "I haven't had company in ages."

Sean was surprised to find he could hear perfectly under the water. To his shock, he realized he was breathing normally, too.

"It's magic," said the fish. "You'll get used to it."

"I don't want to get used to it," Sean said,

beginning to panic. "I want to get out of here."

The fish blinked. "If you had said the right word, you wouldn't be in here at all, you know," it said. "You might as well make the best of it."

"You mean there's no way out?" Sean asked.

"Not until somebody comes along and melts the ice," the fish said. "But that could be a long time."

Sean shivered. "I hope not," he said.

THE END

Continued from page 87

Sean went for the first door. He put the key in the lock, and the door swung open.

But on the other side of the door, he saw only the Sorceress's garden. His heart sank.

"You have done well up to this point," the Sorceress said. "Such a pity."

Sean turned to see the Sorceress standing right behind him.

She held her left hand in front of her face, palm up, and blew gently. Sean smelled her sweet breath as it floated toward his face.

Then he blacked out.

When he came to, he felt strange. He couldn't feel his arms or legs. In a panic, he looked down.

And saw a long stem and two green leaves.

I must be dreaming, Sean thought. *It's got to be a dream.*

The Sorceress knelt down in front of him. He saw his reflection in her pink eyes. His head was a round flower blossom with two eyes and a mouth. His body was a flower stem. She had turned him into a flower!

"Now you are part of my beautiful garden," said the Sorceress. "That is better than going home."

"Nooooooo!" Sean screamed.

THE END

Continued from page 118

Sean checked the time and date on his computer. The portal had worked perfectly. It was like no time at all had passed in the real world while he was in Liasa.

When Sean woke up the next morning, he headed to the junk shop after breakfast with the book under his arm.

When he entered the store, he heard the sounds of an argument. A boy and a girl stood in the center of the store, yelling at each other.

"It's mine!" shouted the boy.

"I saw it first!" the girl yelled back.

Sean shook his head. If those kids knew what kind of freaky stuff was in this shop, they might not be arguing over it. He thought about telling them but decided not to. They'd just have to find out for themselves, like he did. In fact, he had an idea that this was what the Scream Shop was all about.

Sean proceeded to the counter. He put the book on the table and looked directly into Mr. Cream's green eyes.

"So I guess you know what happened when I read this book," said Sean.

"Of course I do not. It's difficult to keep track of all of my inventory," the little man answered.

Then he eyed the book on the counter. "Would you like to exchange *War of the Trolls*? I have many other books you could choose from." His green eyes twinkled.

Sean was startled. He hadn't thought about taking another book. He'd have to be crazy to take another book from Mr. Cream.

Then again, his adventure in Liasa had been incredible. He wondered what the other books had in store for him.

"Let me just take a look . . ." Sean said.

THE END